The man was naked. Totally naked.

Rising out of the surf on a moonlit night, he was sleek, sexy and obviously unaware that she was there. As he turned toward the water, Maggie was barely able to suppress a sigh. His back was as sleek and muscled as every other part of him.

He stood, his legs slightly spread, and combed his fingers through his wet hair, raking it back from his face. He flexed his broad shoulders, then stretched his arms toward the night sky. The motion was animalistic and oh-so-tempting....

Maggie knew she should leave quietly, that she should be embarrassed about watching him. It was positively hedonistic on her part, and nothing she would ordinarily do. But she didn't leave. Something must have happened to her once she came to this place....

At least that's what she'd thought...until he lowered his arms and, without warning, turned in her direction....

Dear Reader,

Every one of us knows that there's that special guy out there meant just for us. The kind of guy who's every woman's fantasy—but only one woman's dream come true. That's the kind of men you'll meet in THE ULTIMATE... miniseries. Whether he's the man who'll follow you to the ends of the earth or the type to stay right in your backyard and promise you a passel of babies, the men you're about to meet are truly special. We hope you enjoy all the wonderful stories and fabulous men coming to you in THE ULTIMATE... series.

Regards,

Debra Matteucci
Senior Editor & Editorial Coordinator

Books by Mary Anne Wilson

HARLEQUIN AMERICAN ROMANCE

495—HART'S OBSESSION
523—COULD IT BE YOU?
543—HER BODYGUARD
570—THE BRIDE WORE BLUE JEANS
589—HART'S DREAM
609—THE CHRISTMAS HUSBAND
637—NINE MONTHS LATER...
652—MISMATCHED MOMMY?
670—JUST ONE TOUCH
700—MR. WRONG!
714—VALENTINE FOR AN ANGEL

Rich, Single & Sexy

MARY ANNE WILSON

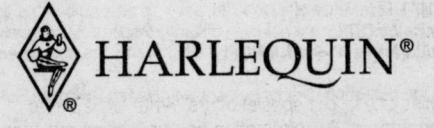

HARLEQUIN®

TORONTO • NEW YORK • LONDON
AMSTERDAM • PARIS • SYDNEY • HAMBURG
STOCKHOLM • ATHENS • TOKYO • MILAN • MADRID
PRAGUE • WARSAW • BUDAPEST • AUCKLAND

ISBN 0-373-16760-1

RICH, SINGLE & SEXY

Copyright © 1999 by Mary Anne Wilson.

Chapter One

Maddox, California

When the phone rang at midnight, Maggie Palmer
was curled up on a chaise longue in the living room
of her tiny bungalow several blocks from the ocean.
Reading a book about the area just south of the main
Caribbean islands, she was dressed in jeans and a
white sweatshirt, with her bare feet tucked under her.

In the low glow from a side reading lamp, she
stared at one glossy page on which a full-color picture of a pirate was captioned "Sebastian Lake, aka,
The Terror." The artist had fashioned an image that
was overwhelming in every respect. The pirate possessed towering height, a solid body under a blood-
red long coat and black britches, a wild black beard,
a terrible scar at his temple, and a fierce look in his
black eyes.

"The Terror, indeed," Maggie muttered, looking
away from the dark eyes as she reached for the por-
table phone sitting on the side table.

"Hello," she said into the receiver.

A voice from her past, which had popped back into
her life a week ago, came over the line. Amanda. "I

was just about to hang up. I figured you weren't there, or that bank manager boyfriend of yours was there with you.''

''Assistant bank manager,'' Maggie said absent-mindedly as she turned in the chair and touched the coolness of the hardwood floor with her bare feet. ''Amanda, do you have any idea how late it is here? It's midnight.''

''Oh, sorry,'' she said with no discernible trace of being sorry. ''Apologize to whatever his name is. I didn't mean to interrupt anything.'' Amanda actually giggled, and for a moment it could have been seven years ago, in the college dormitory, with the two of them gossiping about life and men. It could have been…but it wasn't.

''Bill, his name is Bill, and he isn't here,'' she said as she stood and headed toward the back of the house to her darkened bedroom. ''Actually, I was reading.''

''Reading?'' She sounded horrified. ''You're supposed to be packing.''

Maggie sank down on the edge of her bed, laid the book she was carrying on the white comforter and reached to turn on a small side light. ''I told you I didn't think I could go.''

''But, you said you'd think about it, and we've only got a few days. Please, tell me you'll go. After all, how many times do you turn thirty and have the party in paradise?''

She looked at the closed book near her side, at the dustcover with the images of the area in full color, and it was so very tempting. ''I was just reading about the area, and the history of it, and I've been thinking about—''

"Don't think. Don't read about it in a book. Just do it. Live it. You and me, together for our birthdays. It'll be like old times—drinking cheap wine, talking into the night, telling each other our deep, dark secrets—but no term papers. What more could you want?"

"Cheap wine? What's the matter, have the Pharrs lost all their money?"

She intended that as a joke, but Amanda wasn't laughing. "Okay, so we'll have expensive wine," she said a bit tightly.

Maggie frowned at the tone of Amanda's voice. Amanda had married John Pharr right out of college, the youngest son of Armand Pharr, a man who had founded a dynasty built on oil. After the wedding, Amanda had dropped out of Maggie's world and fallen into a life of privilege and luxury that Maggie could only imagine. There had been Christmas cards, the odd phone call here and there with promises to get together "sometime." But that had never actually gone beyond the "what-if" stage, until a week ago, when Amanda had called with her offer.

They'd get together to celebrate their mutual birthdays at the Pharr compound on the tiny island of St. Pelan in the Caribbean. A simple suggestion for Amanda. Pick up and go. But for Maggie it was complicated. She had a job, responsibilities and was about to turn thirty. And then there was Bill Rome.

She'd known him most of her life. They'd both grown up in Maddox, a tiny coastal community halfway between Los Angeles and San Francisco, and they'd started dating seriously a year ago. Now she knew he was going to propose soon. He hadn't had to say it. It was there, unspoken. He was just waiting to make his move.

She closed her eyes tightly for a moment. They were good together, comfortable, easy, even. She liked that and she liked Bill. She admired him, and that was a good foundation for a marriage. At least, she thought it should be. But that didn't stop that niggling uneasiness about making a lifetime commitment, and that's what marriage would be for Maggie.

"Amanda," she said with a sigh. "There's so much going on here, and I've got a lot of…well, a lot on my mind right now."

"Listen, you need this. I need this. Besides, you know we've always been able to talk to each other about anything. So, you can talk to me and I can talk to you, and maybe we can make sense out of our lives. How does that sound? Talking in paradise."

Tempting, but not sensible. "It sounds good, but—"

"No buts. Just do it." Amanda hesitated, then said softly, "The truth is, I need to see you and talk to you." She took a soft breath. "You know what? You're the only real friend I've ever had. I miss you."

She could hear the old Amanda in those words, the girl who was uncertain, even scared about life, and it made her feel uneasy. "What's going on?"

She sighed deeply. "I'm just trying to convince you to accept my birthday present to you, a getaway and a chance to take some time for yourself, a time to shed your image, even if it's just for a few days."

"What image?" she asked. "I don't have an image."

"Sure you do. Sane, sensible, conservative and predictable."

Maggie grimaced at that. "Please," she muttered as she opened her eyes and looked at her reflection in the hanging mirror over the dresser across from the bed. She grimaced at herself and Amanda's words. "That sounds horrible."

"No, it's fine. It's you, but don't you ever just want to get a bit crazy? Don't you ever want to break free, to live a fantasy, to do things you'd never do in Maddox?" She exhaled. "If you plan on marrying that assistant bank manager, don't you think you need some time for yourself before you settle down? Like an early stag party."

That made Maggie laugh, and it felt good to really laugh. Maggie couldn't remember the last time she'd done that. "Women don't have stag parties."

"Okay, wrong choice of words. But you know what I mean. And it's my present to you, so you can't refuse."

She stood and crossed to the dresser to get closer to her reflection. Maggie Palmer. Sensible, conservative Maggie Palmer. A change for just a few days? To live a fantasy? Her resolve was slipping. "I don't have any clothes or anything, and I—"

"Are you still the size we were in college?"

"Yes, but—?"

"Then we can do what we used to do. You can wear my clothes, and I've got closets full of clothes down there. You can help yourself."

Maggie touched her hair, the wild chestnut curls skimmed back smoothly off her heart-shaped face into a tight knot. Her green eyes were narrowed be-

hind the lenses of her reading glasses, and the freckles on her nose stood out even in the dim light.

"I've got my job here."

"I'm sure you have tons of vacation time. Or call
in sick, then let your hair down and live."

Maggie slowly tugged the pins out and shook her
head until the curls were free and wild, falling down
past her shoulders. As she slipped off her glasses and
stared at herself in the mirror, she felt something in
her click. Suddenly, she wanted desperately to take
some time for herself, to talk to Amanda and figure
out what she was going to do with the rest of her
life. Also, she thought, it would be nice to do something impulsive just once in her life.

"Okay, you win, I'll go," she said, not taking her
eyes off her image reflecting back at her. "Just tell
me where to meet you to fly down with you."

"I'm still in Paris, and I have to take Shari to
Mom's in Vermont so they can take her camping.
Why don't we just meet on the island at the house?
I told them to expect us in three days, so why don't
you go down there, and as soon as I get Shari settled,
I'll meet you."

"I can't do that."

"Of course you can. Go on down, and I should be
there when you get there, or soon after, depending
on how long it takes to settle Shari at Mom's. The
staff will be expecting you."

Staff? This was way out of her league. "Okay,
what do I do when I meet this 'staff'?"

"Do? Let them wait on you. It's their job. Do
whatever you want. The staff knows that the people
who own homes down there cherish their privacy.
Hell, they guard it the way Fort Knox guards the

gold, probably more so. They use their places there
to have privacy, to do what they want, when they
want, and with whom they want without any outsid-
ers annoying them, most notably the press and gawk-
ers. And the staff is there to make sure it stays that
way."

"Okay, I'll try to remember that, and I'll try not
to embarrass you."

Amanda laughed at that. "You couldn't do that if
you tried."

"I sure won't fit in," she said.

"I'll tell you a secret. You'll fit in if you just act
as if you own the world. Plus, everyone will think
you're either a Pharr or with the Pharrs, and that
opens every door there is on the island. That'll even
get you into the Fortress, the main gathering place,
a club that was built on the rubble of a pirate's
castle."

"Sebastian Lake's?"

"You *have* been reading about the place, haven't
you."

She reached for her glasses and slipped them on
as she moved back to the bed and the book she'd
left there. "They mentioned that his place was destroyed in his last battle."

"Well, it's not destroyed now. It's fantastic. Go
and check it out if you get there before me."

She sank down on the bed and pressed one hand
to the bright cover of the book. "I'll just stay put at
your place until you get there."

"Oh no you won't. Don't waste a minute of your
time there waiting for me. Get wild. Find that Maggie who can lose her inhibitions and have fun. Forget
about being a librarian, about your assistant bank

manager and being so sensible. Go swimming, have margaritas, dance naked on the tables at the Fortress.''

"Amanda!''

"Maggie, one of the rules on the island is you never worry about anyone questioning what you do. They wouldn't dare judge one another down there. There's no justifying anything to anyone.'' Her voice was tinged with sudden flatness. "Especially if you're a Pharr.''

"So, I'll pretend to be a Pharr for a few days,'' Maggie murmured.

"Sure, a long-lost cousin. The Pharrs have a ton of shirttail relatives. You're cousin Maggie, and you can do whatever you want to do, and weave any fantasy you want. Get an attitude.''

Weaving fantasies, doing her own thing without having to justify it and having an attitude. Three very foreign things to Maggie. She lay back on the bed and stared up at the shadowy ceiling over her. She was suddenly more than a bit tired of the old Maggie and all the restrictions and pressures on her. "Okay, I'll have an attitude, act as if I own the world and not justify anything.''

"Good girl,'' Amanda said with a laugh. "I can't wait to see this wild and crazy Maggie on St. Pelan.''

Maggie closed her eyes tightly and excitement began to stir in her. "I can't wait, either,'' she whispered.

Two days later
Long Island, New York:

WHEN CONNOR MCKAY WALKED into the master suite of his sprawling mansion at three o'clock in the morning, he was exhausted. Business negotiations for an acquisition of three European companies had gone badly from the word go, and he was frustrated as hell. He walked through the outer room of the suite, and as he stepped into the shadowed bedroom, he didn't bother with a light.

He kicked off his shoes one by one, then stripped off his slacks and shirt, tossing them in a pile on the nearest chair. Dressed only in his Jockey shorts, he crossed to the huge bed which was built into its own alcove and surrounded by windows, and reached for the spread to tug it back.

If he was lucky, he could get three hours' sleep before he had to talk to the offices in Brussels, and he needed every hour of that sleep to recharge himself. He climbed into bed, stretched out his six-foot frame, turned onto his side...and realized he wasn't alone. He touched heat, bare skin, and inhaled perfume that had no business being there.

He jerked back, sprang out of bed and yelled "Fletch!" at the top of his lungs as he grabbed for the light switch.

With the side light on, he was staring at a woman in his bed. A strange woman. Young. With tons of red hair. Pretty in a way, and with the blankets down to her waist. He could see she was wearing a black lace bra that barely contained very large breasts.

She didn't look shocked or embarrassed, but smiled seductively up at him as she patted the bed where he'd been moments ago. "Oh, please, Connor," she said in a husky voice. "Come back to bed. Come on. Let's get to know each other."

"Hell, no," he said sternly. "Get out of here."

She scooted up until she was sitting in the middle of his bed, and now he could see she had on panties that matched the bra. "Oh, come on. Please, I just wanted to meet you, to let you know that I'd do anything for you. Anything." Then she reached behind her and turned to hold out something to Connor. A magazine. *The* magazine that had started all this madness, or at least made it escalate.

She thrust it toward him. "Look. I've got it. I know all about you. Everything."

"Fletch!" he yelled again, and the door crashed open.

An overhead light flashed on, and the woman blinked as she looked past him. Then her eyes widened as Fletcher Jones, Connor's bodyguard, rushed into the room and straight for the bed and her. The man was the size of a mountain, dressed all in black, with short black hair and cold blue eyes. And he was rushing at her like a mad bull.

"Get away from me!" she yelled as she scrambled to her feet on the bed and dove for Connor.

Before she could land in Connor's arms, Fletch had her, lifting her up as if she weighed nothing. The big man had her caught in a firm hold, and he ignored the way she was kicking at him and cursing, questioning everything from his parents' marriage to his intelligence.

"Where'd she come from, boss?" Fletch asked.

"Damned if I know. She was in the bed when I got in it. Get her out of here."

"Oh, Connor," the woman was saying, but she was sobbing now. Tears ran down her face. "I love you. I really love you." Her hand reached out for him, and the magazine dropped to the floor. "Please, let me love you. Please."

Connor looked at Fletch. "Now!"

"I'll call the cops and—"

"Don't tell me, just do it," he said caustically. "This is the third time this month. I didn't think anything could surpass the sky diver, but I was wrong." A million-dollar alarm system, a full security force and a bodyguard the size of Mount Everest couldn't stop a woman who looked as if she weighed a hundred pounds. "How *did* you get in here?" he asked the crying woman.

When he spoke to her, she stopped moving and crying. Her eyes widened, and she actually smiled weakly at him. "I just said I was here to apply for the maid's job, and the man at the gate let me in." She smiled even more. "And here I am."

Connor looked at Fletch. "Fire him, get rid of her, then get back here. We've got some talking to do."

"Sure, boss," the big man said, and as he started to leave with the woman, another man came into the bedroom, one of the guards who patrolled the grounds. "Here, take her down to the back room and call the cops to come for her," he said as he managed to get the struggling woman out of his hold and into the other guard's control. "Trespassing, etcetera, etcetera. And stay with her until they get here."

"Yes, sir," the man said.

"Don't let him take me, Connor," the woman begged as she started to sob again. "I just love you. That's not a crime," she bellowed.

When the guard and woman were gone, Fletch turned to Connor. "I'm really sorry, boss. I'll give orders that anyone coming on the estate has to be cleared by me. That should stop this from happening again.''

Connor reached down to pick up the magazine and stared down at himself on the cover. The photo was of just his face and shoulders, and he'd never even known it had been taken. Along the bottom of the cover, printed in red, a banner spelled out The Ultimate Catch. In a box in the corner, he read, ''Billionaire businessman, Connor McKay, 39, not only drives his rivals mad, he also drives the women mad. Full story on page 100.''

He stared at the picture. Thick black hair, worn a bit too long to suit most conservatives, was parted just off center and had a touch of curl where it brushed the collar of a white shirt. Deep brown eyes, which some said could look right through them, were narrowed and dominated a face that he'd always thought was pretty ordinary. Hardly the ''ultimate catch,'' unless you added lots of money and lots of power. The greatest aphrodisiacs around, he conceded bitterly. And, add to that, he was single. Very single.

There'd been women who'd come and gone, but none that he'd wanted to stay. His last girlfriend had said his mistress was his work, and she'd probably been right. No woman had ever given him the rush and pleasure that winning in business brought to him. They were a diversion, not a necessity, and he liked it that way. But that didn't stop women from reading the article and thinking they could be the woman to change him for good.

He would have laughed at that, if he'd felt any humor at that point. But he didn't. None. He was fed up. All of this craziness distracted him and took his attention away from the important things, like getting Alex Gunner, head of Protomey Tech, to agree to the terms of a takeover.

"Damn it all," he muttered as he tossed the magazine across the room, not caring where it landed. "Since that damned article came out, my life's been a living hell, and it's costing me."

"Yeah, it's like waving strawberries in front of donkeys. And when it comes to the weirdos and the greedy, well..." Fletch shrugged. "A pretty tough price to pay for being who you are."

"Yeah, tough, and way too high right now. This can't go on."

"I know. We'll tighten security, and like I said, I'll have all visitors or prospective employees go through me."

"Tighten security, but I'm not staying here." He raked his fingers through his hair. "I need a place where I can work on this deal without this happening again. I can't even go to the offices without someone showing up there. And thinking I can check into a hotel without some idiot leaking it is out of the question."

"How about the place in Miami?"

"No, that wouldn't be any better than this place."

"Then how about the compound on St. Pelan? It's quiet, security's good. No one gets on the island unless they belong there, including the press. A sanctuary, if you need it."

He'd all but forgotten about the place. He'd bought it five years ago for business entertaining and a tax write-off. He'd never thought of it as a sanctuary before. "That's possible," he conceded.

"You've only been there, what, two or three

times? You may as well get your money's worth out of it, and now seems like as good a time as any to do it."

Fletch was right. Suddenly it seemed like a safe harbor where he could negotiate, concentrate and have security. "Good idea."

"When do you want to leave?"

"As soon as we can transfer all of the files and get the office there operational. In two or three days, probably."

"Okay, just tell me what you need."

"Tell Beatrice to cancel the interview with Don Sanders tomorrow, too. Get all of the paperwork on Gunner. Make sure the office at the house is set up for us and…" He looked at the mussed bed and caught a hint of the offending perfume. "Send a maid up to remake this bed."

"Right away," Fletch said.

"Connor!" His name being screamed startled him as it echoed through the house, coming up from the bottom floor.

Fletch hurried out of the room while the screaming escalated. "Connor! Connor! Don't let them take me!" the determined woman shouted. "Please, you can make them stop. I love you! I love you! Don't make me leave. I know you want me. You love me!"

Connor exhaled as the screams got more and more distant. Then they were gone altogether and Fletch came back in the room.

"Sorry, they were taking her out and used the front doors instead of the service entrance. She's gone, boss. Relax."

Even with that woman gone, he knew there'd be another one to take her place sooner or later. Prob-

ably sooner. "Change of plans, Fletch. I'm not waiting two or three days. I'm getting out of here now.
Get the jet ready, and we'll work on everything on
the way down to the island." He looked at his watch.
"With any luck, we'll be set up down there by
noon."

"Sure seems a shame to be going down there to
a place some might call Paradise just so you can
work," Fletch mumbled.

Connor shrugged and crossed to the dressing area
to get his clothes. "We've all got our own versions
of paradise." He looked back at Fletch. "And right
now, mine is being able to work and not worry about
some strange woman ending up in my bed."

Chapter Two

One day later
St. Pelan

It was midnight and the man was naked. Totally naked.

Right then, Maggie knew that she'd come across one of the locals, someone who didn't need to justify anything to anyone. Especially rising naked out of the surf on a moonlit night, sleek and sexy and obviously unaware that she was there—partially hidden by a rock outcropping—staring at him.

He was no more than thirty feet away from the rocks that came down the side of the twenty-foot bluffs and into the shallow surf. Talk about attitude. He reeked of self-confidence, and the sense that he belonged anywhere he wanted to belong. He looked as if he felt he owned the world.

He was lean and sinewy, at least six feet tall, with the shadows cast by the partially full moon hiding nothing about him. Not the dark hair slicked wetly back from his strong-jawed face, nor his broad shoulders. Not his smoothly muscular chest, nor his flat stomach that looked rock hard or...the fact that he wasn't wearing anything at all.

Damn it, despite the fact that the tepid water was swirling around her ankles and she was wearing only a pink string bikini she'd borrowed from Amanda's wardrobe, Maggie could feel heat rising in her. Water trickled off her hair, down her back and between her breasts, and she didn't realize how tense she was until she felt the rocks biting into her hand where she gripped them for support.

She eased her hand on the rough stone but kept watching the man as he moved onto the sand. His back was to her now, a strong, sleek back, as muscled as every other part of him. Then he stopped, his long legs slightly spread, and he combed his fingers through his wet, shoulder-length hair, raking it back from his face.

Maggie couldn't take her eyes off him as he turned slightly toward the water again, and she was barely able to suppress a deep sigh. He was sleek with water, defined by shadows and with his attitude firmly in place. He tipped his head back, lifting his face to the night sky, flexed his broad shoulders, then stretched his arms up, hands over his head. The motion was animalistic and tempting, making the heat in Maggie deepen.

She knew she should quietly leave, that she should be embarrassed about watching him like that. It was positively hedonistic on her part, and nothing she would have thought of doing back home. But she didn't leave. Something must have happened to her once she'd stepped onto this island. Some of the attitude was definitely rubbing off on her. At least she thought that...until he lowered his arms and, without warning, turned in her direction, his face etched by moonlight.

For a flashing moment, it felt as if his darkly shadowed eyes were looking directly at her, that he'd discovered her spying on him. Any attitude she'd thought she'd had was shattered at that moment, and she acted exactly as the sane, sensible Maggie from Maddox would have acted. She jerked back, flooded by embarrassment, and got ready to run. But she took only one step before catastrophe struck.

The rocks shifted under her feet, and, before she knew it, she was falling backward, her arms flailing around her. Then the impact came, with water splashing everywhere, getting into her mouth and eyes and leaving her struggling to right herself.

She scrambled awkwardly to her knees, then got to her feet, spitting water out of her mouth and swiping at her stinging eyes. So much for her having an attitude and acting as if she owned the world. If she'd done that, she would have met the man's gaze, dared him to say or do anything, then left when she wanted to, on her own terms.

But, no, she'd turned to run and ended up in the water, floundering around like some beached fish. Now she was standing, fighting the burning in her eyes and hoping against hope that he somehow didn't know she was there. She just prayed that she hadn't screamed when she fell. She couldn't remember if she had or not.

If she had, maybe he hadn't heard her. Maybe he hadn't heard the splash. Maybe all she had to do was get back to the Pharr house and lock the door. Maybe she could die from embarrassment in private so that by the time Amanda got here, they could have a good laugh about her spying on a naked man at midnight in paradise.

The next instant, all of her foolish "maybes" were shattered. She knew someone was there at the same time she heard water splash and a hand catch her by her upper arm. This time she knew she screamed, because the sound hadn't died out before she was jerked around to face her worst fears.

The naked stranger, still gripping her arm, up close and very personal, was just inches from her. She clapped her free hand over her mouth to shut off any more screams, and kept her eyes up, not daring to look down that expanse of naked chest…and lower. If he'd been compelling from a distance bathed in moonlight, he was overwhelming this close.

She looked into eyes that had been all darkness from a distance, and were just as dark up close. Yet the impact of his gaze was staggering under dark brows, as staggering as the details she could see in the moonlight. High cheekbones, a strong, clean-shaven jaw with a slight cleft, and a wide, sensuous mouth tight with anger.

For one stunning moment, she thought she knew him. That proved she was totally crazy at the moment. If she'd ever met this man, naked or clothed, she surely wouldn't have forgotten. His hold on her hovered just this side of real pain, and a muscle worked in his jaw as she stared up at him. No, there was no way she would have been able to forget a meeting with him.

"Who in the hell are you?" he demanded in a deep, rough voice. A drop of water trickled from his dark hair and down his temple, but he ignored it. "And what are you doing on this beach?"

Maggie slowly lowered her hand, took a breath and tried to think. She could go with her first impulse, which was to tell him the truth. She could tell him she was out for a midnight swim, spotted him naked, stayed to watch him. A simple answer to a simple question. But that idea died under the burning intensity of those dark eyes. No, there was no way she could humiliate herself that way with this man.

She knew right then what she was going to do. Just what Amanda had told her to do. She'd act as if she belonged, as if he were in the wrong, and that she was angry and upset with his high-handed behavior. *Attitude is everything.* If she had to have attitude, she'd have attitude. After all, this was her week to do whatever she wanted to do.

She jerked back from him, knowing she'd be forcing him to either physically restrain her or to let her go. She was thankful he let her go, that she didn't have to fight him to get free. Then she realized that when he moved back and she moved back, she'd be looking at him…at all of him.

For a moment she almost closed her eyes, but in a flash she realized that he wasn't naked now. Relief made her feel slightly light-headed. He'd put on light-colored shorts, which were now spotted darkly from the water on his body. Still, the sight of his naked chest was making her mouth go slightly dry. She swallowed hard and gathered up her ''attitude'' again.

When she spoke, her voice was tight and harsher than she'd intended, but with some firmness in it. ''Who do you think you are, grabbing me like that?'' she demanded.

''I'm asking the questions here,'' he said tightly,

not backing down a bit. "You're trespassing, so if I were you, I'd do some explaining and do it fast. Unless you want to explain it all to the police."

The police? Good heavens, her attitude obviously wasn't any match for his. "Trespassing?" she asked in an annoyingly weak voice.

"Damn straight. This is a private beach and it's mine. Now, what are you doing on it at this time of night watching me?"

So, he did own the world. At least this very exclusive piece of it where he could swim any time and any way he wanted to. She fought the urge to rub the spot where he'd grabbed her arm moments ago, and she felt a twinge of anger. He acted as if he was the center of the universe, not just the owner of the world.

He came a step closer but didn't touch her again. "So, are you going to explain to me or to the police?"

"I didn't know it was private," she said testily, her new attitude firmly back in place. "And I hardly think we need the police. I'm not armed."

His eyes flicked over her and she felt that heat again. Finally, he conceded, "In that suit, you can't hide much, I'll give you that. But convince me not to call the police," he said. "Tell me why I shouldn't."

She nervously tucked her unruly, damp curls behind her ears, fighting an urge to cross her arms protectively over her breasts. "Because it's ridiculous." She touched her tongue to her lips, which still tasted of saltwater. "Besides, it's not neighborly to be calling the police just because I stumbled onto this part of the beach without knowing that it was private."

"Neighborly? What are you talking about? How did you get down here, anyway?"

"I came down some steps in the bluff where I'm staying." She motioned in the direction of the Pharr estate. "Right next door—at least, the next house. It's maybe half a mile or more, but it's the next one for sure. So, that makes us neighbors."

"You're from the Pharr place?"

"Yes," she said, feeling a bit more confident as the anger appeared to diminish from his voice.

She heard him release a rough breath. "You're a Pharr?"

"A distant cousin," she said, though she wasn't at all easy with the lie.

Connor didn't endure confusion well, and right then he felt very confused. When he'd come out of the water, it had taken him a minute, but he'd begun to sense someone there. On a beach that was supposed to be totally secure, he'd turned and caught a flash of movement, then heard a scream and a splash, followed by sputtering sounds.

It wasn't Fletch. He'd left him at the house, and he was probably sleeping by now. Besides, the big man moved silently, appearing without any warning. The sounds coming from behind the rocks had been anything but covert. Then he'd found her, just getting to her feet, dripping with water and scrubbing at her eyes.

For a flashing moment, he'd thought she was the best of the lot—a leggy, slender woman with high, small breasts, wearing a bathing suit that was little more than a few strings and bit of material. Then his anger had exploded and he'd gone to her, grabbing her, and, barely having time to register how soft and warm she felt in his hand, he'd jerked her around to face him.

She'd looked shocked, with a riot of damp curls framing a face that had delicate features touched by the moonlight. Now she was here in front of him, and he had to concede that she really was beautiful, maybe more so than the others. And she wasn't crying or screaming or calling him by name and saying she loved him.

She was right in front of him, looking a bit annoyed while she told him she was a Pharr. She had lifted her slightly sharp chin a fraction of an inch and pushed her hands behind her back. He had to admit, if this was a ploy, it was one that hadn't been used on him before.

"So, you're a distant cousin of the Pharrs?"

She nodded, but not too enthusiastically. "I said I was." She lifted her chin a bit higher. "I am."

He was so tired of the whole stalking business that a part of him just wanted to believe her and let it go. But he couldn't. There was something about her, something out of place, and he couldn't define it. "So, the whole family's down here. Jack, Amy, Gwen?"

She frowned at him. "You must have the wrong family, or you don't know the Pharrs' correct names."

He watched her carefully, wishing that the moon wasn't shadowing her eyes and partially hiding her expression. He prided himself on being able to read a person's expression, but with her, it was hopeless. "What do you mean?"

"You must be referring to John, Amanda, and

goodness knows who you mean by Gwen, unless it's John's mother, Gloria?''

"Yes, of course that's whom I was referring to." He studied her. "Are they all down here, too?"

"No, just me, and Amanda's coming in tomorrow sometime."

He relaxed even more, and as he did, something in him stirred. He watched the way she touched her tongue to her lips, and the way she tipped her head to one side when she looked up at him. Damn it, she was appealing. For the first time in a long time, he was looking at a woman with a touch of lust. It actually felt good to have that, rather than disgust or distrust. "So, you didn't know this was a private beach?"

"I've never been down here before, and no one told me." That chin lifted a bit again, a habit that he found oddly endearing, until she said, "I didn't expect to get attacked, either."

He hadn't expected to find her here, either. "I guess I owe you an apology." That was another thing that he hadn't done for a long time. Apologized to anyone. "I overreacted."

She tucked her curls behind her ears, exposing a slender throat. "You certainly did."

He almost laughed at her response. There was no coyness in it, no teasing. Just a flat statement of fact. The woman was in control. She hadn't even mentioned that she'd seen him swimming naked. He liked that.

"I've had some trouble lately, and when I saw you here, well…" He shrugged, wondering why he was explaining things to her. He never explained his actions to anyone, no more than he apologized. But he

was doing that very thing and kept right on going.
''I thought you were one of the crazies who lurk out
there.''

He didn't know what he expected, but it wasn't to
have her laugh softly, a gentle, endearing sound in
the night. ''So, I'm not crazy if I'm a Pharr?''

''The Pharrs could be loony for all I know, but at
least if you're one of them, you belong around here.''

The smiled died, and he didn't understand why.

''If I'm a Pharr, I'm not trespassing?''

''No, you're still trespassing, but I'll let you stay.''

''Thanks, but don't do me any favors. I need to
get back to the house.''

She went around him, and he turned to see her
wading farther out into the water. He didn't understand what had just happened, and he went after her.
''Hey,'' he called as he scrambled into the water.

She turned, and the sight of her waist-deep in the
water with moonlight touching her curls was breathtaking. ''What?'' she called out.

''Was it something I said?''

She was very still, then, without a word, she turned
and dove cleanly into the low waves.

Connor stared at where she'd been, then saw her
surface just a bit farther out and start stroking parallel
to the shore going south toward the Pharr beach. He
felt frustrated and angry, and he hated being cut off.
He wasn't going to let that happen with her. He never
gave up, and he wasn't about to give up now. Hell,
he didn't even know the name of the woman who
seemed so angry with him.

Without another thought he dove into the water
and swam after her.

MAGGIE SWAM AWAY from the shore and from the stranger, who could anger her with words and make heat rise in her with just a look. It was way too dangerous to stay around him and take the chance of saying or doing something that she'd live to regret. She was okay if he thought she was a Pharr, but if she was just plain Maggie, a librarian with no connections, she'd be nothing.

She swam harder as her anger built, anger at him and his damned snobbery. Anger at herself for letting him get to her. Damn it, he had an attitude that hurt. And a sexiness that was disturbing on such a basic level that she could barely comprehend it. Yes, she had done the right thing by leaving.

She swam furiously until her arms began to feel heavy and she had to stop. When she stopped, she started to tread water, and as she turned, she was startled when something surged out of the water right in front of her. For a heartbeat, she had no idea what was happening…then she knew exactly what was going on. It was him, the stranger, right in front of her, with those dark eyes and a look that made her breathing tight.

She forgot to move her hands and feet, and she started to sink then caught herself and came back up enough to keep her head above water.

"You," she gasped as she shook her head to free her eyes and face of water and her clinging hair.

"Yes, it's me."

She hadn't even known anyone was behind her, she'd been so lost in her own thoughts. About him. "I didn't expect…" She took a breath. "What are you doing?"

He swiped at his face, then looked right at her

again. The moon was on his face, exposing an intensity that she had a hard time dealing with. "Trying to keep up with you," he said.

"Why?"

"You never told me your name," he said.

"You followed me to ask me that?"

"No, I actually followed you to tell you I don't understand why you left mad, but then I realized, about ten strokes back, that I didn't even know your name. So, what's your name?"

He wasn't making this easy. He was disarming, even when he'd said things that had made her feel terrible, and it made it hard to stay angry at him. She almost said Maggie, then changed her mind. No, Maggie wasn't here. Margaret was here. "Margaret," she said, and when she would have stroked away from him to go to the shore, he stopped her dead.

He reached out to her, and the tips of his fingers brushed her cheek. "Now, Margaret, tell me why you're mad at me."

She was stunned by the contact, by a jolt of pure awareness that rocked her. "I…I'm not," she managed to say.

"Don't lie to me," he murmured, his hand shifting to touch her lips lightly, then moving to cup her chin. "You were angry back there, and I want to know why," he said, coming closer.

"No… I…" She touched her tongue to her lips as their legs brushed each other's and she knew she should leave. But his touch was making that impossible. This was far too dangerous for her. What had seemed like a simple lie about being a Pharr now felt

like a millstone around her neck. "I'm not mad,"
she whispered.

His hand shifted, slipping under her wet hair to
cup the nape of her neck with warmth. "Prove it,"
he said in a low, husky voice.

She stared at him, wondering if she was just imagining all of this—the man, the night, the touch. But
she knew that it was no illusion when he came even
closer, his body coming against hers. Then he tugged
her to him, their legs tangled, and he blotted out the
moon as he moved even closer. When his lips
touched hers, any other contact was forgotten.

The feel of his mouth against hers, his taste mingling with the pungency of the saltwater, heat and
need, all tangled up in one explosive moment in eternity. A moment when everything in her life made
sense, when nothing made sense.

She drifted below the surface of the water with
him, falling down and down, lost in the moment,
against his body, his legs around hers, and the feeling
of being in a different world was overwhelming. Not
just a different world, but it was as if she'd slipped
into a whole different life. She was someone she
didn't know. Someone who was clinging to a
stranger, returning passion with a passion she never
knew was in her.

Suddenly they broke the surface, there was air all
around, the heat of his body against hers, and the
urge to cling to him forever was staggering. But as
he eased back, as his lips left hers and she gasped
for air, shock and confusion surged around her.
Whatever spell he'd woven around them shattered
when he murmured her name.

"Margaret."

She was Maggie. Plain Maggie. And this stranger had no idea who he was kissing. No more than she knew who she was kissing.

She stroked back, the feeling of his body gone from hers, and despite the warmth in the water, she felt chilled to the bone. Without a word, she swam away from him, away from his touch and his pull on her. His presence, which made it almost impossible for her to remember this, was all an illusion, a lie.

By the time she got to the shore and hurried up onto the silky sand, she knew leaving him wasn't going to be quite so simple. He was right behind her. She could feel it without having to turn to see him. His presence was a tangible thing, something she wished she could run away from, but knew she couldn't.

When he touched her on the shoulder, she almost jumped out of her skin. This time she was on the right beach, and she spotted the towel she'd left on the sand what seemed an eternity ago. She reached blindly for it, then turned, draping the soft terry cloth over her shoulders and using it as a protection of some sort against his presence.

"Do you always do that?"

"Do what?" she asked, nervously tugging on the ends of her towel.

"Run away."

"I didn't run away," she lied. That's exactly what she felt she'd been doing ever since she'd spotted him coming out of the water. "I'm tired and it's late."

He cocked his head to one side, and she tried to ignore the way the water molded his shorts to his body. "Yes, it is time for bed," he said softly.

A smile played seductively at the corner of his lips, and she prayed it wouldn't blossom into a grin. The heat she felt rising in her face was bad enough just from his mention of bed, not to mention the memory of the kiss washing over her.... "Good night," she whispered.

"Good night, Margaret," he said.

She wanted to ask him his name, but something in her knew that the less she knew about him, the easier it would be to forget him. So she turned from him, but every step she took toward the stairs cut into the bluffs felt awkward and strange. She could feel him watching her, and at the top of the rough stone steps, she fought the urge to look back down at the beach. She hurried across a sea of cool grass to the house, which looked vaguely like a modernized castle.

Arched windows, stone walls and multipaned doors gave the structure a decidedly European flavor. The terraces that ran around the bottom story, blending with a swimming pool and extensive decking, gave an unfettered view of the ocean. She hurried ahead, onto the cool flagstones of the terrace outside the grand room, and as she headed for the open French doors, she decided she should have done what she'd told Amanda she was going to do. Just stay put at the house until Amanda arrived. Now she wondered if she should have locked herself in her room.

Chapter Three

Connor watched Margaret go up the stairs, fascinated by the way the moonlight exposed the swelling of her hips, the elegant length of her legs and the glistening wet curls that clung to her shoulders. His body reacted involuntarily to the images, and he turned as the uneasiness grew within him. He wasn't used to losing control, but she'd brought him precariously close to doing that very thing. The fact that he'd kissed her was proof enough of that danger.

A day that had begun with a crazy woman in his bed had ended with a beautiful woman in his arms. He started toward the water, the idea of a swim to ease a tension that grew with each moment he was alone, suddenly inviting. But as he touched the swirling tide with his bare feet, he heard something behind him. It shocked him at how pleased he was to think she'd come back...until he turned.

She wasn't back at all. A big man strode determinedly across the sand toward Connor. Fletch. The man was like his shadow, always there, but never giving away his presence until he had to. "Boss?" he said in a low voice as he got closer. "I was just about ready to call out the National Guard."

Connor waited at the water's edge as Fletch came closer. As usual, he was dressed all in black, a plain T-shirt, jeans and, incongruously, his ever-present western boots. "Afraid the pirates got me?"

Fletch stopped dead in his tracks. "Old Sebastian Lake would run if he ever met you. No, no worries about pirates getting you." He motioned out to the darkness of the water. "However, the jackals have landed."

"What?"

"I got word that there've been some boats off-shore, and it could be the press. So, being down here isn't a good idea. The press doesn't know you're here, but one glimpse and it's all over."

"Oh, God," he muttered, all the pleasures from moments ago dissolving.

"I went to tell you, but you were gone." He rocked forward toward Connor. "I thought we had an agreement about telling me where you'll be, even if I don't go with you."

Connor almost laughed at his tone. "I needed a swim."

"I thought you might have, but I checked the pool."

"Okay, I needed to swim in the ocean."

"Let's hope the vultures don't have telephoto night-vision lenses, eh?"

Connor frowned at Fletch. Either the man hadn't seen Margaret or he was too polite to mention her. No, he hadn't seen her. One thing Fletch wasn't was polite when it came to strange people being around.

"Figure out how to get them the hell out of here," Connor snapped.

"You've got it."

"Was that the only reason you were tracking me down?" he asked as he began cautiously climbing over the rocky bluff that separated his beach from the Pharrs. Good thing both he and Fletch were in such good shape, or the climb would have been impossible.

"No. You were contacted," Fletch eventually said, breathing heavily as they finally touched down onto Connor's beach.

"When?"

"Fifteen minutes ago."

Damn it. He'd been down here playing when he should have been working. "How does it look?" he asked as he walked with the big man.

"That's not in my job description to figure out if Gunner and Blanc are going to fold," the man commented.

"I didn't know you had a job description."

"You hired me as your bodyguard, a challenging but dirty job, protecting your body from all those women." The man spoke with studied dryness as they neared the perimeter of Connor's beach. "That's why I was relieved you decided to come down here. I get a break. Down here, the Ultimate Catch is just another simple billionaire, blending in with all the other billionaires."

"Just don't let down your guard," Connor muttered as he spotted the stairs up to the house and headed for them. "You never know who'll turn up."

Fletch laughed at that. "Just let me check your bed before you climb into it, if you ever get a chance to sleep again."

Connor took the steps two at a time, not speaking until they had both stepped up onto the grass that circled the outdoor swimming pool and cabana area. "God, I should have bought up all of the magazines with that cover and burned them."

"Even you couldn't do that," the big man said as he fell into step with Connor on the way past the pool to the expanse of terrace at the back of the brick-and-stone mansion. "Bestselling cover they ever had, or so I'm told. Every woman in the world must have bought it, and now they're all there trying to figure out how to throw themselves at you."

Not every woman. The image of Margaret came to him in a flash—her looking up at him in the moonlight, her skin sleek from the water that clung to her, that minuscule bathing suit, the way her breasts rose and fell, high and inviting. But she hadn't exactly thrown herself at him. In fact, he'd been the one pursuing. That was odd in and of itself, but fascinating.

"It's your job to stop them," he finally said.

"Sure is. A dirty job, but someone has to do it," Fletch muttered. "So, don't be going off by yourself. It could get damned embarrassing if some woman started crawling all over you and I wasn't there to peel her off."

Connor couldn't force a smile at the image Fletch was bringing to mind. Margaret might have let him kiss her, but, despite the fact that she was sexier than any woman he could ever remember seeing, she wasn't exactly clinging to him. Except for that one moment when he'd kissed her. But the next moment the situation had shifted again. She'd made him go after her. No, he'd gone after her because he'd wanted to, because he was fascinated by her. She'd barely slowed down for him.

He'd never chased a woman in his life, and he wasn't about to start now. He'd obviously been a bit crazy, maybe from lack of sleep or from being alone too long. He didn't know. And he wasn't going to stand here and figure it out. He had work to do, important work.

"Okay, tell me exactly what the rep for Gunner and Blanc said when they made contact," he asked as he headed into the house and quickly moved toward his offices on the ground floor.

MAGGIE HAD BARELY STEPPED into the garden room near the terrace on the main floor, when the maid, Pauline, silently entered.

"Phone call, miss," she said with a subservient dip of her head. Despite the fact that it was well past midnight, the maid was fully dressed in the dove gray uniform the rest of the house staff wore. "It's the missus."

"Thanks, Pauline," she said as she swept the towel up and around her wet hair to wrap it turban-style around her head. "I'll get it up in my room."

"Yes, miss," the woman murmured, and literally backed away from Maggie with her head bent down.

She had no idea how the Amanda Clinton she'd roomed with in college had assimilated into this world of wealth. It was surreal, with servants and houses the size of museums, where a "guest suite" was as big as her whole bungalow back in Maddox. It wouldn't be easy for her to do it, that was for sure. Then again, she'd never have to worry about that.

No, the wife of an assistant bank manager wouldn't ever have to deal with servants…or strangers swimming naked on the beaches of a tropical island. As she hurried through the cavernous house with its stone walls, quarry-tiled floors and opulent antiques, she almost laughed. If her life worked out the way it seemed it would when she went home, her biggest concern would be dealing with Bill's big family, not worrying about a man who was so sexy it made her ache.

That killed her smile. No stranger should be getting that reaction from her. And a stranger certainly shouldn't have been kissing her. She scrubbed her hand over her lips as she went past rooms and spaces she hadn't even explored yet, then took the stone steps of the sweeping staircase off the entry to the second level. But the action didn't stop that sensation of lips on hers, tasting her, exploring her in the weightlessness of the water. That should have been Bill, but even as she thought it, she knew that would have never happened with Bill.

The hallway, which looked as if it had been carved out of stone, led down to the "west wing," where she was staying in what the maid had called a small suite, a collection of three rooms. She went into the sitting room, which had stone walls, thick blue carpeting underfoot and a lounge facing the view out of doublepaned windows that overlooked the cove below.

Tossing the towel on a chair, she crossed to the low table by the lounge and reached for the phone.

"Hello?"

"Maggie, hello," her friend said over the line.

"Where are you?"

"Still at my parents' place. I'm sorry. I thought I'd be on my way down there by now, but Shari started running a low fever and all she wants is her mommy, and I can't leave as long as she's sick. Not even with her Mamaw. She won't let go of me, and I wouldn't rest if I thought she was sick and I wasn't here."

"She's going to be okay?"

"The doctor said she'll be fine, but she has an earache and it's taking its time getting better. And with John off in Berlin working, she needs me." There was a sigh over the phone, and the tone of her voice when she talked about John seemed rather sad.

"You know, John should have been coming down here with you for your birthday," Maggie said.

"He couldn't take the time." Her voice changed. "Besides, I wanted to have fun. And we're going to have fun as soon as I get down there. But feel free to start the party without me, and I'll catch up when I get there."

"I'll wait to party until you get here."

"I told you to have fun, to do whatever you want, to go crazy and forget about rules."

She'd been doing that on the beach, and she'd only regretted it. "I'll make do," she said.

Maggie heard someone talking in the background, then Amanda said, "You do that. Now I need to get going. Shari's awake. I just wanted you to know that I think I'll be able to fly out tomorrow. I'll call and let you know."

"Okay. See you tomorrow," she said, then hung up.

She shook out her hair and almost went to get a brush to tame the damp curls. Then she thought better of it. She left the curls alone and crossed to the open doors to the outer balcony. She stepped out into the night, into balmy peace and quiet, and looked out over the vast waters below the bluffs. There was a light flashing in the darkness, then it was gone and the night was complete.

She touched the rail and glanced down at the beach. In the moonlight, she could see nothing down there. He'd gone. And she should be thankful. Instead, she felt uneasy and restless. A brief image of the man coming out of the surf appeared, then it blended with another image that she couldn't grab onto and hold. Him. But not in the night or sleek with water, or so close she could feel his breath skim over her bare skin.

That restlessness grew, and she tried to take deep breaths to ease it as she removed her damp suit. Just wait until Amanda found out about the encounter. Or maybe she wouldn't tell her about it. She tossed her bathing suit onto a chair. Okay, maybe she'd tell her some of it, but she definitely wouldn't tell her everything the way she had in college. No, she wouldn't mention the kiss.

She looked off into the distance to the north, where another light was shining, flashing to life in the darkness somewhere at the top of the bluffs. It shimmered in the night, and she knew somehow it was him. His light from his house. She experienced the oddest sense of connection because of the light and it made her nervous. She turned from it and went back inside, but that didn't stop the sense of him not letting her go again.

CONNOR TURNED OFF the bank of overhead lights in the expansive office on the ground floor of the beach house around three o'clock in the morning. He walked through the darkened house to the stairs and up to the master bedroom suite that filled the top floor of that section.

He'd used the shower by the outdoor pool on his way into the house, but right now, he needed hot water and soap and time to just stop thinking. He went into the main section of the suite, turned on all the lights and looked around. It was empty, very empty, and he was relieved.

He went through the sitting area, where a wall of French doors opened to a balcony that extended out and over the pool below. He crossed to the double open doors to the workout room with the bathroom off of it and went inside, stripping off his clothes.

He went right to the huge shower cubicle, turned on the water, then stepped under the steamy spray. He stood very still, letting the water course over him, letting heat surround him, and for the first time in hours, he stopped thinking. At least he did for a moment or two, until the water cascading around him brought back that moment when he'd fallen down into the ocean with Margaret in his arms, kissing her.

He reached for soap and a sponge and moved closer to the water, lifting his face into the spray as he started to scrub himself. His body was beginning to respond on its own to the images flashing through his mind. Soap and water and the roughness of the loofah weren't helping at all. His mind refused to let it go.

He didn't need this. A distraction wasn't all bad, but on his terms. This definitely wasn't on his terms. And a part of him was pretty sure that any man involved with Margaret took it on her terms. He turned off the water and got out, reaching for a towel before he padded back into the main area, turned off the lights and moved to the open doors.

As he rubbed the soft terry cloth over his body, he stepped out into the night and stood on the balcony. Just a kiss. A simple kiss. And it wouldn't let him go. He'd been too long without a woman, that had to be it, or at least without a smart, sexy, sane woman.

Despite the speculations in the magazine article, he'd never bedded a lot of women. If they only knew the truth, they'd probably accuse him of lying. It had been over a year since he'd even been interested in a woman enough to clutter up his life with an emotional connection. And even then, it hadn't been earthshaking. She'd accused him of being too involved with his work, and it had been over before he'd even found out if he really wanted her. When she'd gone, that had been that.

He dropped the towel by his feet and crossed to the railing, gripping the sculpted metal with both hands. Why, when he was in the most important negotiations he'd ever been involved with, had he come across a beautiful woman on the beach at night and gone a bit insane?

He laughed at that. Insanity…well, he had an idea that Margaret could drive a man insane without much trouble. With her bedroom eyes, her lips parted so seductively, her body barely covered by that ridiculous excuse for a swimsuit. Yes, insanity was a definite possibility, he conceded as he turned and went back into the shadowy room.

He crossed to the wet bar by the bedroom doors, poured himself a generous splash of Scotch, not even bothering with ice, and tossed off the drink in one gulp. It burned a fiery path down his throat, spreading in his middle, but didn't do a thing to blot out the insanity or to ease an ache that seemed to be settling into his body and frustrating him to no end. He put the glass down on the bar, then turned, and before he knew what was happening, he caught his foot on something and crashed forward into a table that held a stack of files he'd brought down to the island with him.

He fell to one side, catching himself with his hand on the back of the chair, but that didn't stop the table from upending and the files from flying everywhere. Before Connor could even straighten up, the door flew open so abruptly it crashed back against the wall and Fletch raced into the room.

Fletch was framed in the streaming light from the hallway, a hulking figure in dark shorts and a tank top. "Boss, are you all right?" he demanded, one hand on his side where he carried a small revolver, the other hand reaching to the right of the door frame.

Connor rubbed at the smarting pain in his shin as he blinked at the light that suddenly flooded the area. "Yeah, sure," he muttered as he looked at the papers and files scattered everywhere.

Immediately Fletch crouched down and reached for the mess. "Sorry, boss, I told the maid you wanted these in the office, not up here." He stacked the folders as he spoke. "I thought you'd had another midnight visitor or something." As he put the last of the papers back on the table, he stood and raised one eyebrow at Connor. "Nice outfit," he said dryly.

Connor didn't even bother responding to that. Instead, he turned and headed for the bedroom. He went into the expansive space that was formed by turretlike walls and two stories of vaulted ceiling. He got briefs out of the dresser, stepped into them and, as he turned, noticed Fletch in the arched entry.

"Anything else you'll be needing tonight?" Fletch asked.

Need was a pretty powerful word, and Connor didn't want to even think about the needing he'd felt tonight. "Nothing," he said.

"What time in the morning?" he asked.

"I've got to touch base with Brussels, so I'll be up and going at six."

"Boss, you haven't slept for days, and three hours of sleep—"

He looked at him. "I'm fine. You go and get some rest. Turn out the lights on your way out."

Fletch turned with a nod, and Connor waited for the lights to extinguish, then the outer door to shut before he stripped the linen comforter off the massive pedestal bed. He stretched out on the cool sheets and stared out the wall of windows at the night.

He'd always fallen asleep quickly, a gift he made the most of when he needed to. And sleep did eventually come to him. But instead of having a restful sleep, he found himself lost in dreams that had no beginning and no end...all centering around Margaret.

MAGGIE NEVER WOKE EARLY. If she had her choice, she'd stay in bed until noon. But the next morning she was wide awake when dawn broke. After trying to go back to sleep, she gave up and got out of bed. By the time she was dressed in another of Amanda's bathing suits, a deep blue string bikini, and was stepping down onto the beach below the Pharr mansion, the sky was brushed with a wonder of pastel colors that reflected back off the water. She dropped her towel on the sand, then headed for the water's edge and dove into the warm surf.

Sleep had helped center her, and as she swam out beyond the breakwater, she could finally put last night in perspective. It had all been a blip in time, as insubstantial as a dream. And it was over. She flipped onto her back and floated in the warm saltwater. The sky overhead was brightening, and an occasional bird flew past.

She heard a distant noise and glanced to the horizon. There was a dark shape against the morning sky, a boat that was so far off, it was less than a dot. She looked back overhead, stroked slowly, then flinched when a cramp in her calf startled her. She pushed herself upright in the water, trying to ease the discomfort. When it began to relax, she looked toward the beach and knew it was time to go back in. She glanced at the gray stone mansion barely visible over the bluffs, then slowly swam for the shore.

When she felt the sand under her feet, she stood, waist-deep in water and tested her leg, which still had twinges of the cramp. Then she waded to the shore and onto the silky sand. She kicked something near the shoreline and looked down at a perfect deep pink shell by her foot. She crouched down, lifted the shell and fingered the smooth, almost iridescent shape.

As she stood, she closed her hand over the shell and looked around for her towel, but she couldn't spot it. At that moment, as she turned to look up the beach for it, she realized she'd made a mistake. This wasn't the Pharrs' beach. Although the rough bluffs looked identical, the beach was wider here. When she looked up at the top of the bluffs in the new light of day, she saw a portion of a house.

But it wasn't the Pharr house. It was done in the gray stones, but instead of two stories, it looked as if it soared three stories into the skies. It sprawled out forever on both sides, and looked like a castle, but a castle that was built into the bluffs instead of on them. It was framed by lush greenery and dominated by elegant palms.

Last night she'd wandered onto the wrong beach, but this time she'd swum onto the wrong beach. She looked to the south, not certain what direction she'd drifted. She could see that unless she was up to swimming, she wasn't going to make her escape that way. The bluffs jutted out toward the water, and the surf was high enough on the rocky barrier that she knew she couldn't just wade around it. Climbing over the barrier was also not an option, given the stiffness of her legs.

A rocky barrier. As if the rocks had tumbled from the bluffs and into the water. Her heart dropped. She'd not only gotten on the wrong beach again, she was pretty sure she'd gotten onto the *same* wrong beach again. If she still couldn't feel the cramp in her calf, which threatened to come back if she tensed it again, she would have run into the water and left. But she couldn't.

She looked north at a sweep of beach that seemed to go on forever, but in the distance she could see that the bluffs cut right into the water, making an impassable barrier in that direction, too. She shouldn't be here, but she didn't see how she could make her escape until she spotted stone steps in the granite bluff framed by a weathered iron railing on either side. They cut back and forth in the stone, going upward to the top of the bluffs.

They were one of two options open to her right then. It was a choice between the stairs or sitting right here until she could swim, which might take a while. The phrase *sitting duck* came to her. No, she wasn't going to sit and wait for God knew what or who. It had been devastating enough to run into the man at night, but she had no desire to run into him in the daylight. Naked at night was a far cry from being naked in the bright sunlight.

She turned to the stairs and took a deep breath. If she was very lucky, she could use the stairs and no one would see her. If she could find the road, she could find the Pharr house. She crossed to the steps and headed up. Maybe the worst that could happen would be that she'd run into a servant. The house looked a lot bigger than the Pharrs', and goodness knew, they had enough servants to choke a horse.

Besides, maybe the stranger wouldn't even be here. Maybe he'd left, or maybe he was still in bed sleeping and would never know she'd been back. Bed? That thought brought images to her that she didn't want any part of going on in her mind. She climbed as quickly as she could and got to the top, where the steps were framed by stone pillars on either side.

Cautiously, she stepped out onto the top, into a sweeping area crisscrossed by terraced levels defined by stone walls, rough steps from one to the other, and low-growing ferns and plants dotted with towering palms that swayed in the morning breeze.

She hesitated as she looked further at the house on the highest level of the bluff. It had looked expansive from the beach, but up close it was overwhelming. It was fashioned out of blue-gray stone and spread out so far on either side that she couldn't make out the corners. Balconies at each arched window and door combination overlooked the ocean, and on the lower level it seemed to jut out into the air, framed by a glass barrier.

A castle for the rich and famous, she thought as she looked around at the triform path network. One path led to the left, the second to the right along the very top of the bluff to some sort of lookout point farther down the way, and the third led up the terraced levels to the house. She hesitated, then turned to the left path that wound its way through a thick growth of lush plants and into a stand of swaying palms. Her only hope was that it led away from the house, allowing her to escape without being noticed.

Hope died hard in her when she'd only taken a half dozen steps on the smooth stones before she knew she wasn't alone. Someone was there, but before she could do more than hesitate, hands were grabbing her from behind and an agonizing sense of déjà vu suffocated her.

Chapter Four

Maggie held her breath when her captor jerked her around, but her shock deepened when she wasn't looking into the midnight eyes of the stranger from last night. She was looking into startlingly cold blue eyes that belonged to a man the size of a mountain and dressed all in black, from a plain T-shirt, to black pants and western-style boots of tooled leather. His dark hair was very short, his jaw a bit heavy, and his voice was like gravel when he ground out, "Good God, you women never give up. How in the hell did you get here?"

His grip never eased, and she knew a choking fear that had never entered her mind last night when the other man had captured her. No, last night she hadn't reacted with fear to him being there, or to the isolation, or the darkness, or the fact that the other man had seemed more than capable of overwhelming her.

She almost choked on that last thought. The man last night didn't need size to overwhelm her. He'd done it with a kiss. A much more potent weapon than this man most likely possessed. But this man was scary. His eyes were as cold as ice, and his features extremely controlled, not even reacting when she tried to swing at him with her clenched fists.

"Let me go," she sputtered as her hands found only air. Her struggles were about as futile as the words she was managing to get out. "Let me go, or you'll be sorry!"

At least he didn't smile at her pitiful attempts, but neither did he let her go. "Oh, will I? I've got a feeling you're going to be the one to—"

"Fletch, let her go!"

A shout cut through the early morning air and did what Maggie's fighting and words hadn't begun to do. They made the huge man let her go immediately. As the viselike grip disappeared, she stumbled back, caught her balance and looked past the big man to see her rescuer.

It was him, the stranger from last night. But now she could tell his hair was more than dark, it was almost black, a bit long, slightly curled and falling thickly from an off-center part. And his face, in the clear morning light, was all planes and angles. His skin was tanned and taut, his lean body dressed this time in snug jeans and a silky white shirt open at the throat, with long sleeves caught in at his wrists. Naked, he'd been devastating, but in some way, now, he was even more compelling as he hurried down the stairs from the house and strode across the thick grass toward them.

As Maggie stared at him, she suddenly knew where she'd seen him before. The sudden realization hit her so hard she couldn't even take a breath at that moment. His image was almost painfully bright in front of her as he moved as if he owned every inch of the space he inhabited. And he probably did. No wonder she'd felt as if she'd met him before. They'd never met, and they never would have if she hadn't come here pretending to be something she wasn't. There was no way she would have ever met Connor McKay if she'd stayed in her own world.

She clenched her hands tightly as he neared her, and she was startled by a stinging sensation in her right hand, but that only distracted her momentarily as she came face-to-face with the man. The pictures in the magazine hadn't done him justice. She doubted any picture could. She'd seen the magazine the day before she'd left Maddox, in the drugstore. There'd been a row of covers staring at her by the checkout stand, all bannered with the blaring caption, The Ultimate Catch.

She'd also heard all the rumors about the women in his life, the crazies who stalked him and ran after him, and his hatred of it. He'd never married, was worth billions and was sexy as hell. She'd read that, but now she could personally attest to the fact. So sexy, he could make a woman do things she normally never would. Well, she certainly had last night.

"Boss, she came up the stairs from the beach and I thought—"

Connor cut off the man's words again with a simple motion of his hand as he stopped right in front of the two of them. Now she could see that his eyes were more than brown. They were as dark as the midnight had been when she'd first seen him, and they were framed by thick, short lashes. One of the wealthiest men in the world, and one of the most eligible bachelors, maybe *the* most eligible man anywhere.

A man who was pursued by women everywhere

he went. It all made sense now, his protectiveness of his space, the way he'd grabbed her last night on his private beach, a man the size of a mountain watching for interlopers. And that's just what she was, however unintentional, both last night and this morning.

"And she's welcome here anytime," he said firmly.

"Boss?"

Those dark eyes never looked away from Maggie's, even as the owner spoke to the other man. "She's from the Pharr house. Margaret." His eyes flicked to her lips before meeting her gaze again. "We met last night."

She damned the heat that rose in her face at his words, which brought back the kiss from the night before. A kiss that would have never been offered if Connor McKay had known whom he was kissing.

"I'm s-sorry," she stammered. "I had no idea this was your place." Oh, God, she was explaining everything, justifying being here. Any image she thought she'd been building with the man was surely crumbling with each word she uttered.

"Margaret Pharr?" the man in black asked abruptly.

She forced herself to look away from Connor and turn back to the big man. "I'm—"

"Damn it, this is not acceptable," the big man muttered as if she hadn't started to speak. "None of the reports said anything about a Margaret Pharr being here. It's supposed to be an Amanda Pharr, the youngest son's wife. Down for a week. She's obviously not Amanda. She doesn't look anything like her pictures. Nothing."

"Amanda's picture?" she asked.

"You'd better update your security reports," Connor said evenly.

Security? She looked at the big man and finally saw the bulge under his T-shirt at his waistband. Of course, security. She pushed her hands behind her back. A man like Connor McKay would pay someone to keep eager women away from his boss. "I'm not Amanda, and I—"

"She's Margaret, and she's staying next door. And you need to get back to the house and set up the conference calls for me," Connor said.

The big man hesitated, as if he didn't quite buy his boss's explanation, but he wasn't about to argue with him. Then again, who would argue with a man who was worth billions of dollars? That thought was staggering.

"Sure, boss." He inclined his head toward Maggie. "I am very sorry, Miss Pharr. It won't happen again."

She didn't bother correcting him. "That's okay," she said quietly.

He glanced at his boss. "I'll set up Gunner for nine. Is that okay?"

"Let him call us, and when he does, tell him we'll speak at nine," Connor said.

The big man nodded, then moved away, taking the stairs that led up to the glass-sheltered terrace two at a time.

Maggie stood very still, trying to figure out how to get the hell out of here without looking like a fool. She braced herself, willing herself to be cool and controlled while she made her escape. Then she looked at Connor and was met by an expression that blew all control on her part out of the water. He was smiling, an expression that crinkled his eyes and eased the lines around his wide mouth. The Ultimate Catch? He must have smiled at the person who wrote that line, because that smile was guaranteed to rock anyone's world. It surely rocked her world without even trying.

"Well, alone at last," he said finally.

His voice startled her, as smooth as honey. But being alone with the owner of that voice was the last thing she wanted. No, it was the last thing she could deal with at the moment and the last thing she should be indulging in. There was no way she could keep up this pretense that she was in her element. She'd never been more out of her element, and money had nothing to do with that fact.

She clenched her hands tighter and realized that her right hand hurt. She drew it in front of her, and then heard Connor cry out, "Good God, what did you do to yourself?"

She looked down at her hand and saw blood everywhere, along with the broken shell in the middle of her palm. She jerked her hand up and, as if in slow motion, watched the shell fly out of her hand, hitting Connor in the chest, leaving a bright red stain on the fine material of his shirt before it tumbled to the ground between them.

Connor acted as if he hadn't even noticed it, but kept staring at her hand. When she looked back down at it, she felt real pain and watched blood oozing from a straight cut in the middle of her palm. It was small, barely an inch long, but blood welled out of it. She'd broken the shell in her hand and hadn't even realized it had cut her because she'd been so distracted by Connor.

"Fletch!" Connor yelled, making her jump. "Damn it, that damn shell sliced your hand wide open." He didn't give her a chance to say anything before yelling again. "Fletch, get the hell out here!"

The big man was suddenly there at the glass wall looking down at them from the third tier. "What's going on?"

"Get a first-aid kit and some clean towels. Bring them out by the pool. Now!" he called as he looked away from the wound and up at Maggie. "Maybe we should get a doctor out here."

"No, no doctor. It's just a cut, a small cut," she managed to say in a slightly unsteady voice. She closed her hand gingerly, trying to stop the bleeding. "I forgot I had the shell in my hand." She looked at the offending piece of crustacea by her feet, her blood still bright on it. As bright as it was on Connor's silky shirt.

She was startled to find him reaching out to put his arm around her shoulders. For a moment she had the terrifying thought that he was going to pick her up and carry her up the stairs. Before he could do anything that crazy, she moved away from his support, ignoring how appealing the idea of leaning on him was.

"Can you walk?" he asked.

"Of course. It's my hand, not my foot," she said in a shaky voice, and headed over to the stairs.

Connor strode around her to take the steps ahead of her and led the way up three levels to an opening in the glass barrier. As she took the top step, she emerged into a spectacular area that swept across the entire back area of the mansion, part terrace and part pool and Jacuzzi, and all of it with a marvelous view.

She only glanced at the house, getting a vague impression of the pool being dissected by an expanse of glass set in the stone walls, so that half of the pool appeared to extend into the house. She barely had time to marvel at it, before Connor touched her arm and urged her over to chairs by a large round table made of weathered wood sitting by the glass barrier. He pulled out a chair for her, and as she sank down in it, he crouched in front of her and reached for her hand.

"Come on, I'm not going to bite you. I just want to help," he said, his dark eyes holding her gaze intently. It was foolish to fight him on this, and she knew it. She let him take her wounded hand in his, and she slowly opened her bloody fingers. The wound seemed so small to produce that much blood, but even now it was starting to pool on her palm again.

Then Fletch arrived, standing behind Connor, not saying a thing. He just laid a white metal tin on the table, opened it and reached inside, took out a package, ripped it open, then handed Connor a thick cotton pad. "Pressure," he said, and Connor put the cotton on her hand and then pressed it against the wound.

She took a sharp breath, then bit her lip hard. "Sorry," Connor said, wincing at her pain but holding the pad there for a long moment before easing it back from her palm. The blood had slowed considerably as he tossed the saturated pad onto the table. Cradling her hand, he spoke to the big man hovering over his shoulder. "Give me some disinfectant."

Fletch opened a tiny brown bottle, dipped a cotton swab in it, then handed it to his boss. Connor looked right at Maggie and said, "This is going to hurt, but we need to clean it. Okay?"

She nodded and closed her eyes. Fire brushed across the wound and she forced herself to stay very still. Then it was gone and pressure was applied again. When she opened her eyes, she saw a stark white square lying on her hand. Fletch handed Connor strips of adhesive, which he used to wrap around her hand and fasten the dressing to the wound.

Finally, he smoothed the strips, then rocked back on his heels a bit and she could feel him studying her intently, as he continued to hold on to her wounded hand. She stared down at her hand and his deeply tanned fingers cradling it gently. "How's that?" he finally asked.

Her hand ached a bit, but amazingly didn't really hurt all that much. "It's…it's much better. Thank you."

"Need anything else, boss?" Fletch asked.

"Yes, a drink for Margaret." She looked up at him, meeting his dark gaze as he said, with a slight inclination of his head, "Brandy?"

She was light-headed enough without drinking alcohol at this time of the morning. "Oh, no thanks."

"You're as white as a sheet," he said without getting up. "You need something. Tea, coffee, juice?"

"Juice. That would be fine," she said, and slowly drew her hand back from his to rest it palm up in her lap.

Connor stood and looked at Fletch. "Tell Theresa that we'll have some fresh orange juice with chipped ice out here."

"Right away, boss," Fletch said, then went back

into the house through open doors by the side of the pool.

Connor moved to the chair opposite Maggie and dropped down, sitting forward, his elbows resting on his knees. He was frowning at her. "Are you sure you don't want me to call a doctor?"

She shook her head. "No, of course not. I'm fine. You did a good job." She looked down as she flexed her hand cautiously. "I forgot I had the shell in my hand."

"I hope it wasn't important to you," he said.

She looked back at those dark eyes, narrowed in the bright light of the new day. "I just found it." A clinking sound drew her attention and she looked toward the house. Across the pool a heavyset lady in a dark dress stepped outside carrying a silver tray with a pitcher and glasses on it. She hurried over to where they sat, put the tray on the table and silently poured what looked like orange juice into two tall glasses half filled with chipped ice.

"Mr. Fletcher said you wanted this."

"Yes, thanks, Theresa," Connor said as she turned to hand him the glasses.

With a nod, the woman left, and Connor turned to hand one of the glasses to Maggie. "Maybe this will help."

"I'm fine, really," she said emphatically, taking the glass carefully with one hand, making sure that she didn't touch Connor in the process. Maggie tasted the cool, sweet juice and let it trickle down her throat.

"Mr. Fletcher is your bodyguard?"

"Oh, he's my bodyguard, assistant, sounding board, friend. You name it, he can fill the bill."

She turned from Connor to look at the house, anything to avoid looking into those dark eyes. "This is an incredible house," she said, filling the spaces around them with her voice. "How did you ever find it?"

"Add real estate broker to Fletch's job description. He's the one who found it. He knew what I needed."

"A place big enough to house the population of a small nation?"

He laughed, a wonderfully rough sound in the morning air. "I never thought of it that way," he said. "I just saw it for what it could do for me."

She glanced at him, making very sure she narrowed her eyes slightly to diminish his impact on her. "What's that?"

"Right now, this is the only place I can breathe and not worry about being hounded. I've had some things happen lately, and I assumed..." He shrugged, cutting off his own words.

Sensing his obvious discomfort with the subject, she said something just to divert the conversation. "This place is pretty well protected."

"That's why I was surprised to find you down on the beach. It's not easy to slip past the security, but..." He shrugged again. "Anyone can if they're determined enough to do it."

She sipped more juice and decided that if she was going to continue this conversation, she'd better talk about something that wasn't personal. "Well, it's got natural protection. The shape is like a circle closing back in on itself, and with the bluffs, there aren't too many places for someone to land where they wouldn't be noticed."

"Are you serious?" he asked, looking decidedly taken aback at the information.

She was babbling, but it was safe babbling. "It's a natural fortress. That's why the pirates used it so effectively when they were led by Sebastian Lake. The shape of the island forced the enemy to come in at one of two points, and Lake secured both of them. The enemies were, as they say, sitting ducks for him. He lured them in and *Bingo!* they never knew what hit them."

He sipped his drink while she spoke, then smiled slightly at her. "If he was that good, why doesn't it still belong to his ancestors?"

"You mean, instead of to paranoid wealthy people?" she asked.

He laughed at that. "Okay, why do we have it and his heirs don't?"

"Poor old Sebastian blew it just once, and that one time cost him his head."

"He was beheaded?"

"No, not literally. He was actually hung in the stone archway that was the opening to a cove that he used as his trap for his enemies. It seemed fitting to them to hang him where every approaching ship would see him and be warned off."

"You're a veritable wealth of information about Sebastian Lake," he noted as he eyed her over the rim of his glass. "I'm impressed."

"Don't be," she said, taking a quick sip of her own drink. "What's impressive is this view." She motioned toward it. "And the pool. It's incredible."

He sank back in his chair, cradling his juice in both hands and studying her from under his thick lashes. "I'll tell you a secret."

She didn't want any other form of intimacy with
Connor. Not when she was here under totally decep-
tive circumstances. "I don't think—"

"It's not national security," he said with that
smile flickering in his eyes now. "I've never used
the pool."

"What? You live here and you've never used it?
You obviously swim." She didn't want to think
about him swimming and her being there. "Why
wouldn't you use it?"

"I prefer the ocean." He glanced at the pool.
"Swimming in a pool's boring."

It was her turn to laugh. "Boring? A pool that
most people would die to have in their backyards,
and you think it's boring?"

"I guess I should have said it's ordinary. I've
never gone in for ordinary."

She looked down at her drink, at the chips of ice
shimmering in the pale orange liquid. She was ordinary. Very ordinary. "I guess you wouldn't. This
house certainly would never be called ordinary."

"If we liked ordinary, we wouldn't be where we
are, would we?" he asked softly.

She could feel a trembling in her that had nothing
to do with the persistent aching in her hand. "No,
we wouldn't, would we. And you certainly wouldn't
be in a house like this with a pool you never used."

"Another confession," he said, sitting forward,
holding the glass loosely in one hand and resting his
forearms on his knees. "There are rooms in this
place I've never seen. Fletch said there are about
twenty-one rooms, fifteen baths, and I've only seen
a handful of them."

"You aren't joking, are you?"

"You can tell when I'm joking, because I raise my hand and say 'I'm joking,' so there's no misunderstanding."

He seemed so close now that she had a hard time making herself not push back in the chair to keep some space between them. "How can you live in a house and not see the rooms?"

He fingered the glass, swirling a pattern in the condensation with the tip of one finger. "First of all, I don't live here. I come here occasionally. This is my fourth time in five years. And when I'm here, I've got things that keep me busy."

"You've never just walked around the place or been curious to see what you paid for?"

"No. No guided tours. Do you know every nook and cranny of your homes?"

"I've been in every room of any house I've ever lived in," she said, not adding that it wasn't hard to look through four or five rooms.

He stood as he put his glass of juice on the table and towered over her, blocking the sunlight. It was a very uncomfortable feeling for her right then. "Do you want a guided tour right now? We can explore the house together."

She took a quick sip of her juice, then put the glass on the table and shook her head. "I don't think so." She looked down at her legs and realized that there was blood drying on her skin. Gingerly, she brushed at it and grimaced. "I need to get going," she said, wishing he'd move back so she could stand without running into him.

"Why don't you shower before you leave?"

Her eyes shot up to meet his, and there was something there, a look that she couldn't define, but it definitely made her face feel hot when images of a shower in this house, with him— She cut that scenario off quickly. That wasn't his offer and that wouldn't be his offer. "I can go and clean up at home."

He motioned to a building near the house on the far side of the pool, a place almost hidden by lush plants and vines. "You can't go back to the house like that. Why not clean up in the cabana? I've been in there, and I can guarantee that there's a very workable shower."

She would love to get the blood off her. "I guess I would feel more comfortable," she admitted, and thankfully he moved back so she could stand.

She got to her feet, felt a wave of light-headedness. Connor had her by her shoulders before she realized what he was doing.

"Whoa," he breathed, so close that his breath brushed her bare skin. "Easy does it. Do you need help?"

"No," she said as the world settled and she got her balance. "I'll be fine."

"Theresa!" he called and the maid was there so quickly Maggie suspected that she'd been hovering just inside the house waiting for him to need her.

"Yes, sir."

"Make sure there are fresh towels in the cabana."

"Yes, sir, there are."

"Good." He looked back at Maggie, those dark eyes flicking over her face. "Are you sure you can make it on your own?"

"Sure," she said, and he drew back, letting her go.

She moved past him, crossing the cool flagstone

to circle the pool. ''We'll have a tour of the house when you get out,'' he called after her.

She didn't turn but headed right for the cabana and reached for the door. All she wanted was to shower, then leave. She wasn't good at games, and pretending that she was born to this stuff, that she was blasé about a house the size of Windsor Castle and a pool that went right into the house was more than she could carry off right now.

She stepped into the building, into cool shadows filled with wicker furniture and a frosted cubicle shower. She locked the door, then, without bothering to take off her bathing suit, stepped into the stall. She turned on the water, and as it flowed over her, she held her injured right hand above her head against the tiled wall to keep it dry.

As soon as she was done, she was leaving. There wasn't going to be a tour of the house, or any more shared secrets with Connor. She was simply leaving. She knew the Pharr house was south of here, and she'd simply head south. Alone.

Chapter Five

Connor watched her go into the cabana, and as the door shut, he sank back into his chair. A day less ordinary. He'd expected to wake up, take on Gunner and the conglomerate, start the wheels into motion for the takeover and sit back and watch his machinations come to fruition.

None of his plans included looking down from the terrace to see Fletch with Margaret in a bear hug and her flailing about, ordering him to let her go. He'd thought about her since the night before, about whatever it was that fascinated him about her. But he'd managed to put that out of his mind this morning. Until he saw her. Then she seemed to fill every corner of his mind.

He hadn't been prepared for his reaction to seeing her bloody hand, either. Usually, he was cool in a crisis, no matter what it was. But seeing her standing there with blood dripping from her slender hand, a feeling that was suspiciously like protectiveness had taken over. All he had wanted to do was help her.

That was new to him, too. He reached for his drink and took a long swallow of the cold orange juice, then put the glass on the table next to hers and glanced at his watch. He had over an hour before the calls were to begin. An hour that had definite possibilities. He glanced back at his house, and he realized he'd never really looked at it before. And he'd certainly never wondered about the other rooms, either.

Another first, he thought. A tour of his home with Margaret. Yes, that had definite possibilities.

"Boss?"

He saw Fletch coming out of the house and heading toward him with the cordless phone in his hand. He had his other hand pressed over the mouthpiece, and as he got closer, he mouthed, "Gunner."

The man was trying a preemptive strike, and that made Connor angry. He wasn't going to do this by Gunner's rules or at Gunner's whim. He was going to control this situation. "Tell him I'm..." He glanced at the pool. "Tell him I'm in the pool...with company, and I'll get back to him in a bit."

"The pool?" Fletch said with a raised eyebrow.

"The pool."

"Okay," he said, then put the phone to his ear. "I'm sorry, Mr. Gunner, but Mr. Connor isn't available right now." He listened for a moment. "He's got company and they're in the pool. He said he'll get right back to you."

Fletch frowned, but kept his voice level. "Yes, sir, of course. I'll tell him," he said, then hit the off button. "Polite, but not a happy camper."

"I hope he isn't," Connor said, then looked past the big man as the door to the cabana opened and Margaret stepped out.

Her hair was wild with curls, framing a face with no makeup and freckles that were evident even from this distance. The bathing suit was wet and left nothing to the imagination about a body that was stunning. But beyond the obvious beauty, the woman stirred him. He didn't understand that underlying response, and he hated not understanding things. Especially things about himself.

She walked toward him, her eyes narrowed in the brightness. The white of the bandage stood out starkly against her honey-toned skin. "How are you feeling?" he asked, vaguely aware of Fletch moving away and leaving.

Maggie stopped with a cushion of space between herself and Connor. "Better," she said, then looked past him for a way out of the terrace area. "If you could just show me where the road is from here, I'll be going."

"No, you won't," he said abruptly.

Her eyes darted back to him, and a slight smile softened his abrupt response. "Excuse me?"

"The tour of the house, we've got time."

"You might, but I don't," she said. "I need to get back to the house."

He hesitated, and she knew that the man didn't take no for an answer easily. But amazingly, he didn't argue with her. "Then let me drive you back to your place?"

"How far is it?"

"Half a mile."

"I'll walk."

He looked down at her bare feet. "Are you sure?"

"I'm sure. If you'll just show me where to go..."

He moved closer to her and motioned past the pool. "This way," he said, and fell into step beside

her as they circled the pool and headed for open
doors on the far side.

She'd been right. The other half of the pool was
inside. As they stepped into the house, they were in
a room that was arched in stone; a waterfall at the
far end fell into the pool, where it seemed to flow in
under the wall. She tried not to be too impressed but
couldn't help a long look at the waterfall and the
Jacuzzi on the side of the pool.

It was another world, a world she didn't belong in
at all.

She walked silently with Connor, through the
room, into another area that might have been called
a den in a normal house. But this room was a den-
library-multimedia room all in one, with a six-by-six
foot television screen built right into one wall. She
tried not to stare and kept going, out into an arched
hallway, walking on carpet so thick she couldn't feel
the impact of the floor under her feet. Finally, they
stepped out into an entry that was as big as a small
house.

A fountain with dolphins carved in marble dominated the middle of a black marble floor, and dual
staircases in heavily carved wood swept up to the
higher floors on either side. Connor stepped ahead of
her to twenty-foot entry doors and pulled one open.
"You know, you never told me why you were on
the beach this morning," he said as they stopped in
the open entry.

"I was swimming, and my sense of direction..."
She shrugged and said truthfully, "I got confused."
And that confusion had only increased for her.

He studied her intently, then said, "I wish you'd
let me drive you home."

"I don't want to bother you any longer. Thanks for your help." She turned away from him as she said, "Have a nice day."

Have a nice day? How original, she thought as she walked quickly across a formal porch area, framed by stone pots with meticulously trimmed and shaped plants in them. She had a brief hope that their encounter was finally over and done with, until she realized that Connor was beside her again, matching her stride.

She kept her eyes down as she descended semicircular stairs to a sweeping driveway. She just bet that Connor McKay seldom let anyone get away from him on their terms. As she stepped down onto the brick driveway, she stopped and braced herself to look up at him.

"I told you, I'm fine. I'm going home."

He studied her silently. "So you've said," he replied in a low voice that ran riot over her nerves.

She closed her eyes and took a breath. This wasn't what she wanted, to have this feeling of something about to happen surrounding her. "I thought you had business to take care of."

"Always. But even with business there's a lull from time to time."

"And this is a lull?" she asked softly. He was silent again, for so long she had no choice but to look up at him. That smile was there, but it was a crooked version as he studied her with those dark, midnight eyes. The connection from his gaze was like a touch of fire, and it was all she could do to make herself stand very still and not run for her life.

"I'd never call you a lull in anything," he finally said.

God, she was so far out of her league that it was terrifying. Yet as he stood there, she knew an urge to let plain Maggie slip away, and let someone called Margaret take her place. When Connor reached out to her, Maggie was horrified that she wouldn't be able to do what she had to do. He touched her injured hand, lifted it gently and looked down at the bandage.

"Take care of yourself," he said. "And don't carry shells around with you."

She hoped that he couldn't feel the shakiness inside her, and she held her breath as confusion all but choked her. The man never let her get her balance, both figuratively and literally, and she desperately needed to find it. She didn't need to feel all those sensations from last night's kiss coming back as strong as if they had just happened.

But the woman who had swirled in the waters kissing him last night was there full force, bringing an aching need with her that made no sense at all. "I...I can take care of myself," she stammered.

"Maybe you should let me help out," he said, his eyes narrowed on her.

"Mr. McKay, I—"

"Connor. I think we've gotten well enough acquainted to make this a first-name-basis relationship."

Relationship? No, not that.

"Are you sure you won't explore the house with me?"

"No, thanks."

His hand slowly let hers go, at about the same speed that a frown darkened his face. "You know,

I'm not used to having to beg a woman to spend time with me,'' he said in a low voice.

She almost laughed at that, but the idea of the women he must have been with left a strange taste in her mouth. "From what I've heard about you, you're not the one who has to do the begging," she commented smugly.

She didn't know what to expect from him. Anger? Denial? Indignation? Whatever it was, it wasn't his sudden burst of laughter and responding "Touché."

"I wasn't trying to be funny," she said, feeling the tightness in her own expression. God, she wanted away from this man with flashing eyes and the ability to hold her world in his hand.

"Actually, it's not funny," he said as he sobered. "I'm sick to death of it." The smile was completely gone now. "Do you know why Fletcher attacked you earlier?"

"He thought I was going to attack you."

He didn't smile. "Exactly. The reason I'm down here right now is because I went to get into bed a few nights ago and a naked woman was there waiting for me, a woman I'd never met before in my life. She said she loved me. Begged me to love her."

"It's that bad?"

He raked his fingers through his hair. "Oh, don't get me wrong. I'm not one of those people who has everything, then complains about it all the time. But it's a fact that if you have money, you're a target in more ways than one. You get a front-page story in a major magazine, and everyone gets ideas."

"What happened to the naked woman?"

"I don't know. Fletch took care of it." He exhaled harshly. "And I'm down here hiding out, thankful to be with people who aren't impressed by my money or position."

She could feel her chest tighten with each word he spoke. "Your own kind?" she said, her voice flat in her own ears.

"That sounds pretty awful when you put it like that, but I guess you're right." He flicked her chin with the tips of his fingers, sending a jolt through her. "Isn't that why we're both here?" His finger rested lightly on her skin at her jawline, riveting her as much as his words were piercing her. "In this place, we don't have to worry about game playing and lies when we meet someone, do we?"

Her stomach lurched as he spoke. Game playing? Lies? "No, I guess not," she whispered.

"That's why I want you to stay for a while. I don't have to worry about you, or wonder just why you turned up on my beach, or why you came here this morning."

"I didn't come here...not exactly," she said.

"Either way, it's safe. Do you understand that? You do understand how rare this is for me, don't you? And what a relief it is?"

"Yes, I think I do," she said, and really did. Oddly, she felt sorry for him, a billionaire who had everything, yet there were things that money couldn't buy. Peace of mind, or the ability to be with someone without worrying about any ulterior motives. And that's why she had to get out of there, before he knew she'd lied and fabricated a persona for herself.

"I knew you would," he whispered, moving slightly closer, the soft breeze of early morning ruffling his hair.

CONNOR HAD NEVER considered his life lacking anything until the moment he'd seen Margaret on the beach, and with every contact since then, including bandaging her wound, he knew just how much had been missing from his life. It sounded corny to him, but it was a solid fact, as solid as the feelings the woman stirred in him and as natural as him leaning down to kiss her right then.

Her taste filtered into him, the feeling of her against him was beyond description, and there was heat everywhere, inside and out. The contact was searing and compelling, and for a moment, she responded the way she did in the water the night before. But before he could recapture the feeling, the kiss was over. Abruptly.

She was pushing him away from her. Pushing him away? His eyes flew open, and he saw her stepping back, her uninjured hand pressed to her lips and her blue eyes wide, staring at him in horror. This was all wrong. As wrong as her jerking away from his touch when he tried to reach out for her again.

He drew his hand back, curling it into a fist at his side, and tried to say something to take the edge off of the disturbing sense of loss and bewilderment he was experiencing at that moment. "Your hand's not raised. I don't think this is a joke."

There was no smile from her, just another step back on the driveway. "This isn't a joke," she said in a voice so low he almost couldn't make out her words. "It's wrong."

"What are you talking about?" he asked, then felt his chest tighten at an explanation that came to him in a gut-wrenching flash. He didn't know anything about her, not really, except that she was a member of the Pharr family. For all he knew, she was married or at least engaged or involved. He'd never even thought about that before, and the sudden possibility was disturbing to him.

"Boss, sorry, it's Gunner," Fletch said from the doorway. "He's demanding that you get out of the pool and talk to him."

Her blue eyes flashed to Fletch in the doorway up the steps, then back to him. Before he could say anything else to her, Fletch spoke again. "You really need to talk to him, boss."

Connor stared at Margaret, who was looking at him with wide eyes that held a tinge of something that looked vaguely like fear. That look hurt like hell for him. "Wait right here," he said to her. "We need to talk." What he needed to do was to make sense out of all the craziness around him. "I'll get rid of this guy in a minute."

He fought the raw urge to reach out and just hold her to him for a moment, just to reassure himself that she was real and that there had to be answers to this craziness. But he turned instead, went up the steps two at a time and grabbed the phone from Fletch.

"Bad timing," he muttered to the big man, then put the phone to his ear. "My man told you I'd call you back," he said into the mouthpiece with as much control as he could muster.

"I'm not good at waiting. I need an answer." The voice was grating to his ear and touched with traces of the owner's German heritage.

Connor wasn't in a mood for the game playing right now, and he was as direct as he'd ever been with an adversary in business. "I really don't have an answer just yet. I need to check some details I missed, then I'll get back to you.''

"Don't give me that, McKay. You know everything you need to know. You always do.''

"No one knows everything there is to know," he said pointedly, more of a truth about Margaret than about his business dealings. If she was married or involved…

He let that thought die as Gunner bellowed, "Just give me an answer.''

Connor could barely think about the business right now, the sense of Margaret behind him definitely disturbing his concentration. When he turned, he was shocked at how wrong he'd been. Margaret wasn't there. She was gone. He looked down the driveway just as she walked out of the open gates and turned to the south without a backward glance.

He stayed where he was at the top of the steps, fighting that last look she'd given him—the one where she'd appeared for all the world as if she'd wanted to escape a fate worse than death. Damn it, she probably was with someone, even if he wasn't down here with her. He knew that the idea of Margaret not having a man caring about her was ludicrous. Of course there was a man to touch her and love her.

She was obviously made to be loved—often and thoroughly—and for a fleeting moment, he felt what could have been jealousy for a faceless, nameless man. This was beyond ridiculous. So, he'd kissed her. A kiss was just a kiss. It meant nothing in the bigger picture. Hell, kisses were cheap and easy to come by. He knew that better than anyone.

"McKay!" The voice thundered in his ear and

jerked him back to reality. His reality. Something he understood and understood well.

"I'm hanging up. I'll call you when I have an answer."

"That's not good enough, McKay," the man said. "If you want—"

"If you want me to even consider this deal, leave me alone until I call you," Connor all but shouted into the phone, just before stabbing the end button.

"Do you realize who you just spoke to so sharply?" Fletch asked from a safe distance in the open doors.

Connor glared across the empty driveway, then turned and strode into the house past Fletch and headed for the right stairway and the master suite.

"Alexov Gunner is a pushy, pompous, short-sighted idiot. The man would try the patience of a saint."

"Which you aren't." Fletch spoke as he hurried after Connor up the stairs.

Connor shot Fletch a cutting look at the second-floor balcony, then turned to the right and hit the door to the master suite with one hand. He sent it rocking back against the wall and strode inside, tossing the phone behind him and into Fletch's hands without so much as a backward glance. "Thanks for that reminder."

Fletch was right behind him as he headed for the turreted bedroom area, unbuttoning his shirt on the way.

"Sorry. I've just never seen you get so upset when you're in the middle of negotiations," the big man said. "It looks like you screwed up big time, but that's just how it looks to me. It's probably just one of your new negotiation tactics, isn't it, boss?''

It was new, but it was no tactic. His patience was at an all-time low right now. ''No, sorry to disappoint you, but I screwed up,'' he muttered as he tossed the silk shirt onto the bed and headed for the dressing area and the walk-in closet to get a fresh one. ''Yeah, I screwed up big time,'' he said as he grabbed the nearest shirt and jerked it off its hanger.

As he stepped back into the bedroom, he noticed Fletch standing by the doors. ''So, do you need to talk?'' the bodyguard asked.

Connor pushed his arms into the light blue silk of his fresh shirt and crossed to the windows by the bed. He jerked the shirt up over his shoulders and began to button the front of it. ''Father confessor? That's not in your job description.''

''I'm on my break. I can either go and get a tan, which I don't need, or I can stay here and listen to you. It's up to you.''

During the seven years Fletch had worked for Connor, things had shifted. Right then, Connor knew how much they'd shifted and how right his description of Fletch to Margaret had been. Fletch had become a friend and just about the only person in the world whom Connor trusted completely.

If he had known what to say, he would have talked to the big man. But he didn't have a clue what was going on right then. ''I'm just edgy and Gunner got under my skin. I don't know why, not really. He's always been a pushy jerk, but this time…'' He shook his head. ''Damn it, I should have kept quiet. Or I should have fed him some bull to keep him off my back.''

"You know what they say when things are going crazy and you don't know why?" Fletch asked as he leaned one shoulder against the doorjamb, the phone still in his hand.

"No, what do *they* say?" Connor asked as he turned and started to tuck his shirt into his waistband. "Tell me."

"Cherchez la femme."

"Oh, please," he groaned. "This isn't a joke."

Fletch wasn't smiling when he held up his free hand, palm up, to Connor. "No, hear me out. You were fine when we got here. You had everything under control, despite our forced departure from Long Island because of the incident with the woman in your bed. Everything was going as planned, until you met the Pharr woman." He lowered his hand. "The lovely Margaret, whom I've never even heard of, much less knew was staying right next door."

He knew this had to do with Margaret, but he didn't understand why it should. "You're just upset because you've been proven fallible. You missed something in your security check." Connor smiled at him as he crossed to the bed and dropped down on the side. "How are you going to live with yourself?"

The man didn't crack a smile. "You're not sidetracking me with sarcasm. It's the woman, isn't it?"

"A woman is a woman," he lied, then sat forward. "It's the mess I made with Gunner that's making me mad. If I blew it, I can kiss the whole merger goodbye."

"You can kiss billions goodbye."

"That, too," Connor conceded. "You think I misjudged this whole thing?"

"With the woman?"

That was a given. He'd misjudged everything about Margaret. "I was talking about Gunner and how I've been dealing with him."

The phone rang twice, then Connor motioned to Fletch to answer it. The big man flicked it on, then said, "McKay Tech."

Fletch listened then mouthed, "Gunner."

Connor couldn't hide his shock at the turnaround by the man he'd just yelled at over thousands of miles of phone lines. He never ceased to be amazed by human nature.

"Just one moment," Fletch said, then covered the mouthpiece with one hand. "What do I tell him?"

"How's he sound?"

"He's obviously had a drink or two, and he says he needs to make sure you understand the figures he sent." Fletch shrugged. "He's obviously not comfortable doing this over the phone. You have him at a disadvantage."

"That's the plan," Connor said.

Fletch lifted the phone a bit in Connor's direction. "Do you want to talk to him now?"

"Absolutely not. Tell him I just left, and you don't expect me to be back in contact until, oh, around four our time. That should give him time to stew a bit more."

Fletch gave him an are-you-sure look, and when he nodded, he spoke into the phone. "Sir, he just left, and we don't expect him back until around four this afternoon. You could call him back or—?" His words were cut off as he listened, then he said, "Yes, sir, of course."

He hung up, then looked at Connor. "He asked very nicely for you to call him when you get back."

"He can call me." He could feel some tension leaving him now that Gunner had blinked. "And he will."

"So, what are you going to do until he calls back?"

"I've got those faxes from Instantel to—"

"Done. Gone. I sent them off an hour ago."

"What about Darnel and the bid on the plant in Rochester?"

"Viking called while you were playing doctor and said the bid was withdrawn. Darnel wouldn't agree to the no-compete clause, and you said if he wouldn't—"

"Of course," Connor said with a dismissive wave of his hand. "Then everything's clear until Gunner makes his next move."

"It looks that way. Is there anything you need me to do for you?"

He almost shook his head but stopped. There was something he wanted to know. "Why don't you do your job and find out why your security report was so lacking." The big man didn't show any emotion at the intentional jab. "Find out what you can about Margaret."

Fletch eyed him narrowly, then shocked him by actually smiling. "Well, I'll be damned," he mumbled.

"What?"

"I know she got to you, no matter what you say."

That was an understatement, but not something he was about to admit to with Fletch. "I just want to know who's in the house next to us."

"Sure, sure," Fletch said. "Consider it done. What are you doing until four? Do I need to adjust my schedule?"

Connor had no idea, but the concept of sitting around here idly, waiting until after four, was something he didn't even consider. "Maybe I'll look around this place," he said.

"Why?"

"Why not? It's my place. I paid a small fortune for it. I'd like to see what it actually looks like."

"Let me know what you find," Fletch said, and left.

"Sure," Connor mumbled absently.

He tugged at the collar of his shirt and crossed to the doors. The only thing that surprised him more than Gunner folding like that had been Margaret's reaction to the second kiss. The first kiss had been mutual, very mutual and very arousing. The second kiss... He shut off that memory and the sense of loss he'd felt when she'd pushed him away.

Loss? No, it had to be wounded ego. The Ultimate Catch had been cut dead. Yeah, ego, and his—if you believed everyone around him—was huge. One thing he knew how to do, and he did it well when needed, was to cut his losses. At least he'd always thought he did, until he asked Fletch to find out more about Margaret. What did he want to know, that she was married and had three kids?

The last thing he wanted to know was how well loved she was by another man. The very last thing. He knew right then he was going to cancel his request for more information on Margaret from Fletch. He didn't want to know anything else about her.

Chapter Six

Maggie sank into the warm water in the bubbling Jacuzzi set into the marble floor in the bathroom suite. The sunken tub was right in front of windows that overlooked the ocean, and the sound of the motor was a soothing, low drone.

She leaned back and closed her eyes, but opened them immediately when all she saw was Connor, that smile and the way he'd looked at her. Her walk back from Connor's house had passed in a blur, and by the time she'd arrived back here, her nerves had been shot. Her neck and shoulders had been tight and her hand had ached horribly.

Pauline had insisted on looking at her wound, pronounced it well cleaned and well bandaged, then suggested a hot bath. Maggie hadn't refused the idea. But now she realized it just gave her too much time to think and remember. She didn't want that. She just wished that Pauline hadn't told her that Amanda had called and left a message that she wouldn't get down here until tomorrow. Now she had a full day to spend on her own...and to stay away from the beach to the north.

"Miss?" Pauline called from the bedroom.

"I'm still in here, Pauline," she called, sitting up, being careful to keep her bandaged hand out of the water.

The tiny woman dressed in the gray uniform hurried in carrying a cordless phone. "A call, miss," she said, then lifted a magazine she had in her other hand. "And I found this, too. You asked if we had a copy. One of the girls had it and said she'd loan it to you. But she wants it back."

She wasn't sure she even wanted to look at the magazine with Connor in it, but she knew she would. "Tell her thank you for me."

"Yes, miss."

"Is it Mrs. Pharr on the phone?"

"No, miss, it's Mr. Pharr."

She took the phone with her good hand. "Hello?"

"Maggie? What are you doing there?"

"Waiting for Amanda."

"Where is she? I called the Paris flat and they said she'd left there yesterday with Shari, but they didn't know where she went. I thought since Shari's out of school right now and she didn't come back here to New York, that she might have taken her down to the island."

This didn't make sense. Amanda hadn't told John where she was going or that she was at her parents' place? "I'm sorry, I just thought you couldn't make it, so I came to keep her company on her birthday."

"Damn it, her birthday," he muttered in a low voice. "Things have been so crazy here. I need to talk to Amanda right away."

"She was supposed to be down here with me now, but Shari got sick, so—"

"Shari's sick?" he demanded. "What's wrong with her?"

"An ear infection, I think."

"Is she all right?"

"Fine, I think. Amanda called last night and said she was at her parents' place in Vermont. They were going to take Shari camping while Amanda came down here. But Shari got sick, and Amanda didn't want to leave her until she was sure she was okay. You can reach her at her parents' house. She's still there. I thought she would have told you where she was going."

There was crackling silence, then John said in a flat voice, "We haven't talked about anything for two weeks. Amanda was in Paris with Shari to take some time..." He exhaled. "Never mind. That's not important. I just couldn't find her, and I didn't know where to look when she wasn't in Paris. I think I'll skip calling her folks' place, though. That might not be a good idea."

"John, I didn't know there was any trouble. I'm sorry."

"Don't be sorry. Things happen. Fairy tales don't last forever." She could hear him speaking in a muffled voice, as if he had his hand over the receiver, then he was speaking to her again. "When you talked to Amanda, did she say when to expect her down there?"

"She's not coming down until tomorrow. Just in time to celebrate our birthdays. She mentioned something about a party at the club, but—"

"When's that?"

"Tomorrow evening."

She'd barely gotten the words out when he said,

"Thanks," then the line clicked and the dial tone sounded. She pulled back the phone, looked at it, then handed it to the maid.

She'd been more than correct that things weren't right with Amanda and John. That saddened her, especially when she had been there at the first, when there had been magic and love. When the fairy tale began. What saddened her even more was John saying, "Fairy tales don't last forever."

She shivered despite the warm water. Fairy tales. That's exactly what she'd almost slipped into last night and this morning when Connor had kissed her. A fairy tale. Now it was over before it had begun.

"Miss?" She looked up at Pauline, who was holding out a terry-cloth robe to her. "Are you ready to get out?"

"Yes, thanks," she said, getting up and slipping on the robe, then wrapping it around her.

"The mister is okay, ma'am?"

"He was just wondering when Mrs. Pharr was going to be here." She crossed to the dressing area and opened the cupboard where she'd hung her own clothes and a few that she'd found in Amanda's closets, a series of storage areas that were big enough to house a small family.

She took out a sundress that was probably very expensive, despite the fact that it looked deceptively simple. It was made of a soft ice blue material, with a halter neck, a low back and a softly pleated skirt that fell to mid thigh.

"Ma'am, will you be going in for lunch?"

She turned with it in her hand. "Going where for lunch?" she asked.

"The Fortress, ma'am, the club. When the missus

called to have things readied, she had us confirm the standing reservation for lunch there. The terrace table. Quite lovely, and a big favorite with the missus and mister when they're down here.''

The place they'd built over the pirate's stronghold. That sounded like a great diversion for her. ''Yes, I think I might.''

She smiled brightly. ''Wonderful, miss. Shall I call and notify them you'll be there around one o'clock?''

''Yes, that would be fine.''

The maid started across the dressing area into the bedroom. ''I'll notify Marin, the chauffeur, to bring the car around at a quarter to the hour.''

''Thank you, Pauline.''

''Yes, miss,'' the woman said, then looked at her hand. ''Would you like me to find you a smaller bandage for your hand?''

She looked down at the large white bandage Connor had put on her hand and decided that getting rid of the bandage might not be a bad idea. ''Yes, please, I'd appreciate that.''

Pauline turned to leave, then stopped and came back to Maggie. ''Oh, and there's the magazine,'' she said, pointing to the vanity. ''That's really something, isn't it? Mr. McKay being on the cover like that, and him having a house next door.'' She smiled at Maggie. ''The Ultimate Catch, indeed. I tried to tell Marilyn, the girl who had the copy, that the women reading that don't know they don't stand a chance.''

''You know Mr. McKay?'' she asked.

''Oh, me, miss? No, I've never met the man, but I've talked plenty to his security man. I've heard that Mr. McKay just doesn't look at any woman who isn't…how can I put this? She has to be like the others, you know, like you and the missus. In his world. He's not about to look twice at a woman who's middle class or…'' She grinned. ''Or someone who's a maid, like Marilyn.''

''No, I guess he wouldn't,'' she said, her voice sounding flat to her. No more than he'd look twice at a librarian.

Pauline motioned to the magazine. ''I can sure see why he'd make women fantasize, but that's not the way it really is,'' she said. ''You know, I heard he dated that actress a while back. Now, what is her name?''

The last thing she wanted to do was gossip about the women Connor had been with. ''I'll be down in a bit.''

''Yes, miss,'' Pauline said, then, with a fleeting glance at the magazine, she left.

Maggie stared at the magazine from where she stood, and across the distance, she could see Connor's face on the cover. Even from that distance, she could feel the impact of the sight of him on her. *I can see how he'd make women fantasize,* Pauline had said. She shook her head, so much like the ''other women'' who read that and had those thoughts right then that it was almost painful.

She crossed to the vanity, intending to get ready for lunch, but when she was going to reach for lotion, she hesitated and ended up touching the magazine. She flipped it open, found the article on Connor, then looked down at the interview, one part catching her attention right away.

McKay admits that he's dated a variety of women, ranging from actresses to doctors.

When asked what are the most important qual-
ities he's looking for in a future mate, McKay
will only say that he has no lists, but he usually
dates women who are comfortable in his world,
whose backgrounds match his. He's "not being
a snob, just practical."

When asked the all-important question about
love, McKay smiles and says, "Love? Sure,
who doesn't want love? But contrary to popular
belief, you choose who you love, you don't let
love choose you. And, if you're smart, you
choose very carefully.

Maggie let the magazine fall shut, then she looked
into the mirror over the vanity. *Women who are comfortable in his world, and whose backgrounds match
his.*

"That about rules you out completely," she said
to her reflection.

She reached for the brush, forgetting about her injured hand until the action of gripping the brush
caused her pain. No matter what she did, she couldn't
seem to ignore the man's existence. She tugged the
bulky bandage off, tossed the dressing into the waste-
basket by the vanity and looked at the wound. Small,
so very small to have bled so much, or to have drawn
a man like Connor McKay further into her world.

She almost laughed at that. Connor McKay in her
world? No, never. A man like that didn't even know
about her world. And he never would. She didn't fill
even one requirement on his list.

TWO HOURS LATER, CONNOR was in a wine cellar he
never even knew existed, and that was where Fletch

found him. The big man could barely stand straight in the low-ceilinged room as he stopped beside Connor at a rack partially filled with reclining bottles of wine.

"I always thought you should flesh it out with more whites," the man muttered as he glanced around the wooden-walled room. "But, all things considered, it's an impressive collection."

"You knew about this place?" Connor asked.

Fletch shrugged. "It's my business to know about everything going on around here. Speaking of which, she's down for a week and single and her last name is Palmer."

"What are you talking about?" Connor asked.

"Miss Margaret, as Pauline calls her, or Margaret Marie Palmer, is down here for a week and is waiting for Amanda Pharr to show up for a birthday blowout. Seems they both have the same birthday."

He'd forgotten to call Fletch off, and now he was glad it had slipped his mind. "Last name's Palmer?"

"That's the last name Pauline had. She also said she's single and, despite being wounded, is heading to the Fortress for lunch where the Pharr table is being held for her. She's also a big fan of Sebastian Lake. She brought some books down with her and has been talking to the staff about the pirate."

Connor wasn't about to tell the big man how impressed he was with how fast he'd gotten the information, or how relieved he was that there was no husband in the picture. "That's it?" he asked.

"I could walk on water for you, I guess," Fletch said with a straight face. "But instead, I'll tell you that the maid, Pauline, likes Miss Palmer. The help will tell everything about everyone, if you ask, even when they don't know they're giving you information."

Fletch knew just about everything about him, and probably some things he didn't even know about himself. "She opened up to you, I take it?"

"I'll get more when I can. Now, what're your plans until four?"

"What would you suggest?"

"I think a good meal's in order, and I hear that the Fortress, despite the fact that you hardly ever show your well-publicized face there, has a table for you." He lifted an eyebrow inquiringly. "I clean up well, if the occasion warrants it."

Connor flicked his gaze over Fletch's black tank top and shorts. "No tux, but something a bit more dressy than shorts."

"You've got it. Meet you in half an hour at the car?"

"Half an hour," Connor said, then Fletch turned and left.

Connor ran a hand roughly over his face, wondering why he suddenly felt lighter and less tense. And that fact had nothing to do with his deal with Gunner and the conglomerate starting to come together. No, he had to admit that it had everything to do with an auburn-haired woman whose look could make him forget just why he was down here in the first place.

"SEBASTIAN LAKE LIVED here for ten years, ma'am," the waiter, a middle-aged man named Hill, said as he poured a goblet of white wine for Maggie. "Right up until his last battle. Then he hung high above the cove before he was buried somewhere on the island in an unmarked grave. There were no services for his soul, that's for sure.''

Maggie knew most of what he was saying, but she enjoyed hearing the spiced-up version that the locals believed. ''No grave marker?''

''Nothing. Some around here think he was cremated and his ashes scattered at sea, so he'd never be on the island again.'' The slender man with close-cropped gray hair and a deep, bronzed tan that was stark against his all-white uniform straightened with the wine bottle in hand. He nodded to the ocean far below the terrace that jutted out over the bluffs. ''Seems fitting. Legend has it that he sat up here and watched for his victims on the horizon, then lit lanterns to lure his prey into the cove. They'd get in, high tide would come, and they'd be trapped. Then old Sebastian would move in for the kill.''

Maggie looked around the terrace, a sweeping expanse fashioned of rough stone against a building that looked as if it had been weathered by the elements for centuries. The Fortress's turrets, narrow arched windows, ornate gas lamps and smooth, worn stones gave the structure an aged feeling. The castle-like building soared into the clear blue sky, but it was hardly a pirate's den anymore. Now it housed the rich and privileged.

''Have you ever been to the caves?'' she asked, fingering the cool condensation on the elegant water goblet Hill had set in front of her.

''No, ma'am. I'm not a very good swimmer, and it's a bit dangerous if high tide comes while you're there. Even if the tide's low, it's pretty dangerous on the rocks. Most around here don't go there at all. But if you're in a boat, you can go right in through the arch easy enough. That's why the crews on the ships thought they'd found paradise—until Lake attacked.''

Maggie looked up at Hill as he meticulously set gleaming silverware in front of her. ''Doesn't it seem odd that they'd have a celebration of the man's last stand?''

The man raised one eyebrow. ''They love the legend around here. Probably because there's a bit of the cutthroat in some of them, if you know what I mean.'' He colored slightly when he realized what he'd said. ''Oh, I'm sorry, ma'am. I shouldn't be talking on and on like this.'' He stood back. ''Will that be all?''

''Yes, thanks,'' she said.

She watched Hill walk back into the main part of the club and almost turned back to the view, but was stopped by the sight of Connor suddenly materializing in the soft sunlight as he stepped out onto the terrace. In an open-necked black shirt with full sleeves and tight black pants, for a fleeting moment, he looked like a pirate. The breeze ruffled his dark hair when he lifted his head as if surveying his domain. Then he turned in her direction.

No, he wasn't a pirate, just a man who always seemed to explode into whatever space she was inhabiting. A habit that was starting to make her feel very uncomfortable in more ways than one. It made her heart lurch in her chest when his eyes found hers, and her whole body tightened uncomfortably. She eased her sore hand onto her lap when she realized it was aching more because she'd clenched it when he'd appeared.

Damn it, he didn't even look surprised seeing her,

but, then again, she was sure that there wasn't much that surprised this man. Fletch was right behind him, all in black, too, like a shadow of a shadow, and when Connor motioned to him with one hand, he came close for a moment. Connor spoke to him, then Fletch went back into the main structure.

Maggie was vaguely aware of the others on the terrace, people who had seemed totally into their own worlds at their tables until right then. Now they were looking up, but not staring, only casually glancing in a subdued sort of greeting. There was no gushing, just a general acknowledgement that the man was there. For a fleeting moment, she wondered who he was here to meet, then that thought was gone as she realized he was walking directly toward her table. As she held her breath, he stopped at her table, then casually touched the back of the chair across the table from hers.

His strong hand pressed into the high leather back, but his eyes were on her. "I always thought the Pharr table out here was the best one they had."

"It's lovely," she said.

"You look good. You've got nice, healthy color in your cheeks."

She swallowed hard, knowing full well it was his sudden appearance that had put the color there. "What are you doing here?" she asked in a voice that sounded like a stranger's to her own ears.

"I'm hungry. Starving. Ravenous." He turned, motioned to the waiter, then pulled out the chair without bothering to ask her if it was okay. "How about you? Are you hungry?"

She watched him take the seat opposite her as if he owned it, and knew that the hunger in her had nothing to do with food, and everything to do with this man. How was it possible to remember every single contact they'd had in the past day, yet she couldn't remember when she hadn't known him. That was crazy, as crazy as her letting him think she was one of his kind.

She wasn't even close to his kind. Connor McKay owned the world. He took the seat at her table, ordered a glass of wine from the waiter standing by, then turned his smile on her. Yes, he owned the world, and Maggie had a feeling he owned any woman he met.

She blinked rapidly, trying to soften the edges of his image across from her. But try as she might, nothing dulled the way his hand fingered his wine goblet. The strong fingers, the dusting of dark hair, the square nails. Fondling, that was what he was doing to the crystal. She looked away, up to his face.

His dark eyes were narrowed, but that didn't lessen the strength of what those eyes could do with a direct look. "So, are you hungry?" he repeated almost seductively.

There was no way she could stop the heat that touched her face again. "I didn't ask you to sit down," she said, her teeth slightly clenched.

He didn't look angry or embarrassed. He just sat there, watching her with those amazing eyes. "Sorry, that was rude of me. May I join you?"

"If I said no, would you leave?"

"Probably not."

"Do you have a clue about what it means to give up?"

"No, I never have in this lifetime."

Short of having the waiter remove him, which she

doubted he would do even if she asked him to, she knew her choices for getting rid of him were very limited. She could tell him the truth, have him look at her with disgust and leave. But one look around the club, then back to his dark eyes, stopped her. She couldn't do that, not here, not with the Pharr name attached to her. And not with the possibility of this turning ugly. She pushed that idea away. This would end, and she would leave, and he'd never know about her charade.

Her only real choice right then was to stay quiet, keep her dignity, try to grab at some sense of peace…and stop looking into his midnight dark eyes. But after just a few moments, she knew that was impossible, too. So, she was left with forcing herself to breathe in a reasonable manner while she clutched at the knowledge that this would end sooner or later.

"How's your hand?" he finally asked.

"Fine, just fine," she said, stopping herself before she clenched it again.

"Is it all right if I ask you something else?"

She exhaled and looked up at him again. He looked so relaxed, sitting back in his chair, one hand resting flat on the stark white of the table linen. A strong hand. And it didn't help that she remembered the way it felt when he'd held her hand as he'd doctored her cut. "What is it?" she asked abruptly.

"Why didn't you wait while I took that call?"

She looked down at the gleam of silver on the table. "You were busy. I needed to go."

"I asked you to stay."

Her eyes shot back to his. "Have you ever heard of free will?"

Her words were tight, but the man took no offense

at all. In fact, he seemed to find her question funny.
The shadow of a smile played at the corners of his
mouth as he said pointedly, "Oh, most definitely.
Nothing's fun if you know that the other person
doesn't have any choices. Where's the challenge in
that?"

"And you love challenges?"

He sat forward, his elbows resting on the tabletop
and his fingers pressed together to form a tent. He
stared at her hard over his fingers, his dark eyes re-
fusing to let her look away as he whispered, "Definitely."

Chapter Seven

Maggie knew she was no match for this man. Verbal
sparring had never been her strong suit, and with
him, it wasn't even an option. "The person who was
on the phone must be an incredible challenge."

"Gunner? No, he's an annoyance at the moment."
He flicked this Gunner off with few words. "He's
also too predictable. That's boring."

She looked away, not certain what to say, or if he
wanted her to say anything. Maybe he just liked the
control, knowing that he was affecting her, and that
she had no cutting retort or some terribly witty pro-
nouncement for his enjoyment. "You get bored easily?"

"No, I don't let myself get bored."

For a moment Maggie had the thought that Connor
McKay and Sebastian Lake could have been one and
the same. Men who felt they owned the world they
inhabited, men who did as they liked, damn the consequences. Men she had no way of understanding
and men she had no business even trying to figure
out.

Something bounced across the table, startling
Maggie out of her thoughts, and she saw a small gold

coin bounce against her knife before it stilled on the white tablecloth. She looked up and Connor was staring at her, his eyes narrowed and one hand pressed flat on the tabletop.

"You're sitting there lost in thought, so, a penny for your thoughts," he said.

Maggie looked back at the coin and realized it was a real penny. "A gold penny?" she asked.

"A lucky penny," Connor corrected.

She pushed it back toward him. "You don't have to pay. You could have just asked."

He ignored the penny. "Okay, what are you thinking about?"

"Sebastian Lake," she said, a partial truth.

"The guy's been dead over two hundred years, and you're thinking about him on a day like this for the second time?" That smile was there, shadowing the corners of his mouth. "A potent ghost, I have to say."

"The waiter and I were just talking about him." She motioned a bit nervously with her good hand toward the building. "After all, this was his place."

"So I heard, and now it houses the paranoid rich."

"People he'd probably welcome with open arms, if he was still here."

"So he could pillage and plunder?"

"Probably. He certainly didn't live by any rules."

"You like that type, a rogue?"

"He wasn't just a rogue, but a law unto himself."

"Pirates usually are their own law," he stated matter-of-factly.

"Sebastian sort of made up the rules as he went. He killed a man in England in a fight over the man's wife, and he paid big money to someone to smuggle him out of the jail the day before he was to go to the gallows. From all accounts, he stowed away on a ship leaving for the West Indies and ended up, someway, with Garçon Spray, a so-so pirate who never really made it big. But when Spray was killed, Lake took over his men and his ships and fell into the pirate life as if he'd been born to it. The rest was, as they say, history.''

Connor watched her intently as she spoke. ''How did he find this place?''

''He stumbled on it when he was escaping from a particularly nasty pirate, Jonas LeVrey. He hid in the cove, let LeVrey leave, then he took over the island and used it as his home base from then on.''

''Any little Sebastian Lakes running around the place?''

''No children, but he had three wives, possibly one at a time, but more likely they overlapped one another's tenure.'' She shrugged. ''The man was not particularly moral in any aspect of his life.''

''You've only been here for a few days, yet you know more than people who have had houses here for years. You could start a Sebastian Lake library of facts and trivia.''

Maggie cringed internally and took a long drink of her cold water. As she put the goblet back down, the waiter arrived with her lunch. Connor sat quietly while the man in white tossed the perfect Caesar salad for her, then as he withdrew, Connor sat forward, resting his elbows on the table.

''Are you that well versed in everything?'' he asked.

''I read voraciously, and I have a mind that just seems to absorb useless trivia,'' she admitted. ''I tend to absorb anything I read or hear. All sorts of things that I'll never be able to use.'' She picked up her fork with her left hand and awkwardly pushed the salad around on the gold-trimmed plate. ''It's never going to make me millions, that's for sure.''

''As if you'd need to make millions,'' he said.

Her fork dropped with a clatter on the plate, and she reached for it quickly. ''Sorry,'' she muttered, and stabbed a lettuce leaf. ''I'm not left-handed.''

Thankfully, the waiter came over to Connor, carrying a bottle of wine, which he presented with a slight flourish. ''From Mr. Bensonia,'' he pronounced, and nodded toward a table by the low stone wall of the terrace dining area. ''With his best wishes.''

Maggie glanced across at a portly gentleman sitting at a table with two younger women. As Connor turned to look behind him, the man lifted the glass in his hand in Connor's direction, an act Connor acknowledged with a slight nod before he turned back to Maggie.

''Pour it,'' Connor said to the waiter, then looked at Maggie. ''Enjoy it. The man has great taste.''

''Bensonia, as in Euro-Bensonia Technology?'' she asked.

''Yes. Now, there's trivia that pays off, knowing who your family is dealing with in business. I heard about the merger with their Italian branch and the Pharr outfit in Dallas. Nice move,'' he said admiringly.

''Yes, very nice,'' she muttered, without a clue as to what he'd been saying.

Hill was there again, placing dishes in front of Connor. When the waiter withdrew, Connor ignored the lavishly presented seafood and reached for his wineglass. He sipped some of the rich ivory liquid Bensonia had sent over, then looked at Maggie over the rim. "So, you're here for a vacation?"

Small talk did little to ease her tension. Maggie looked at the lettuce on her fork and knew she couldn't eat anything. "Yes."

"Did you say you haven't been down here very often?"

"No, I never did say that, though it's true." She laid her fork on the plate and reached for her wineglass.

"Are you staying long?"

"No," she said before taking a drink of the white wine that was as smooth as silk in her throat.

"I admire a good talk show host."

That made her hand jerk slightly. "What are you talking about?"

"They can interview anyone, get those dreaded yes-and-no answers, and still keep things going. I'm not that good. I tend to get crazy when I'm not getting any feedback."

Crazy? He was the one who drove people crazy. She certainly wasn't crazy. "I wasn't aware this was an interview," she said, sipping more wine.

He put his wineglass down and rested his elbows on the table once again. "It's a getting-to-know-you sort of thing. And I can't get to know you if I'm getting yes-and-no answers to everything, no more than you can get to know me."

The idea of getting to know Connor was infinitely appealing, but she made herself hold back that thought. She didn't need to know any more about him. "I'm having lunch, Mr. McKay, and I—"

"I told you to call me Connor."

She shrugged. "I was going to say that I'm having lunch, not interviewing for anything."

"Okay," he conceded, reaching for his silverware. Silently he started to eat, then looked at her and motioned with his head to her food. "You said you were having lunch. Eat. The food here is excellent."

Her stomach was in knots now, and eating was the last thing she wanted to do. Instead, she sipped more wine, then sat back. "Do you ever take vacations?"

He glanced at her. "I'm here, aren't I?"

"And you're working, from what I've seen and heard."

He took his time cutting a piece of fish, spearing it, then eating it before he looked back at her. "Okay, I'm working while I'm here." He picked up his wineglass again and took a sip, then he put it back down. "I'm not a person who can just kick back and do nothing."

"That's obvious."

He fingered his wineglass stem. "Oh, is it?"

"You don't even know the rooms in your own house."

"Actually, I do. At least some of them. Just this morning, after you left, I came across a wine cellar I didn't know I had."

"You didn't know you had a wine cellar?"

"I assumed I did, but I never went looking for it." He speared more food, but hesitated before putting it in his mouth. "It wasn't important to me."

"Priorities?"

"Exactly."

"And work is priority?"

He frowned slightly before popping the fish into

his mouth. He chewed slowly, then finally sat back a bit. "You make that sound bad."

"No, it's not bad," she said, ignoring her own food completely to sip a bit more of the wine. As she glanced at him over the rim of the crystal, she said, "You come to paradise to do work. That's not bad. It's just crazy."

"It's effective," he said. "I'm only available on my terms, and the people I'm doing negotiations with don't know why I'm here. They assume that I'm down here because I'm not that concerned about the pending negotiations."

"You didn't sound unconcerned with that Gunner."

"A minor slip. But I have it all under control for now. He's doing what I want."

"Mind games?"

He nodded. "If you want to call it that, yes."

"And you're good at mind games, aren't you?"

He frowned slightly. "That sounds less than flattering, too."

She pushed her plate back and dropped her napkin over the barely touched salad. "I imagine that anyone who got to where you are in the business world would think it's an asset."

"But I hear disapproval in your voice?"

"It just seems exhausting to always be playing mind games."

"You believe in complete honesty?"

That struck her hard. Complete honesty? Hardly. "No, just being less complicated about things."

"Life's too short?"

Life was too short to sit here with him, feeling her stomach knot and a heat smoldering in her that

wasn't going away. She couldn't fall into the trap of
thinking she could sit and talk with him and get away
unscathed. It wouldn't happen that way. She motioned to the waiter, and the man was there before
she put down her hand. "Yes?"

"I think I'm finished."

The man snapped his fingers and servers were
there, quickly clearing the table on Maggie's side.

"What are you doing?" Connor asked.

She glanced at him as she stood. "I'm done and
I'm leaving as soon as I get the check."

"They don't bring checks. It's on the books."

She felt her face grow hot again. "Of course it is.
I...I was talking figuratively."

He looked at her intently, then motioned her to sit
down. "Give me a minute longer?"

"I really—"

"Just one minute?"

She hesitated, then sat back down, but on the edge
of the seat. "Okay, one minute."

"You don't like mind games, so I'll be as direct
as I can about this."

She didn't like the sound of this, but nodded.

"I've been doing things lately that I'm not used
to doing, and this is one of them. I'll tell you the
truth, plain and unvarnished, for what it's worth."

She clutched her hands and her wound began to
ache. But she didn't ease the fist. Somehow the pain
gave her a bit of focus that she needed right then.
"You know, you don't have to say anything or do
anything. I need to get back to the house and I think
it's better if I just leave now."

He spoke as if she hadn't said anything. "The
truth is, I came here because I found out you were

having lunch here. That's the only reason I came, to see you and make sure you were okay." He shrugged, setting down his glass. "Plain and simple, I wouldn't have come here unless I wanted to see you again and talk to you."

"You saw me, and we talked," she said in a small voice. "I'm fine, and I need to go."

When she would have stood again, he moved quickly, getting up and moving around her before she got completely to her feet. They faced each other in the noon sunlight, and Maggie knew if she inhaled too deeply, she'd be lost. She didn't want to be filled with the scent of this man, which carried on the warm air. Not that, not when she feared that his taste could still be on her lips if she touched her tongue there.

"I'm not done," he said tightly, in a low voice.

"And you're not used to people walking out on you, are you?" Maggie asked, striking out for self-preservation.

A muscle jumped in his jaw, but his voice stayed low and even. "What in the hell are you afraid of?" he whispered.

You and me, she wanted to say, and my lies, but she couldn't. Instead, she looked down and murmured, "I'm leaving."

"I know you aren't married, and neither am I. We're here now, at the same time, and I'll be damned if I'll let you tell me that there isn't something going on between us."

She closed her eyes tightly, a pain in her middle that had no name and more than matched the pain in her injured hand.

"Just tell me that you don't feel it, too, and I'll back off."

There were lies, and there were lies. And this was one she couldn't tell. But she had to stop this, right now, before she got in so deeply, she destroyed herself getting out. Then she knew. Simple. The truth or, at least, a near truth. She braced herself and looked up at him. She had to try twice before she could force out words that she prayed would push him away.

"I...I'm not married," she managed to say in a tight voice, barely able to meet his dark gaze and hold it. "But there *is* someone and we...we're going to be married."

He stared at her, his expression giving away nothing, but it was in the eyes. The way they narrowed, the flash in them that could have been anger, or something else. She didn't know. She didn't want to know. "But you're not married yet."

"No, but—"

"Then it doesn't mean anything," he said. "Everything's up for grabs."

She snatched at anger out of desperation, anything she could find that she could push between herself and this man. "Well, I'm not up for grabs. Sorry."

"Don't be too sure about that."

The anger grew, anger as much at him as at herself. She should have hit him. She wished she could, but she couldn't, not in this place. So, she struck out with words. "You egotistical, stubborn, conceited, arrogant jerk," she accused in a low voice. "What gave you the idea that I'd want anything to do with you?"

"Remember, I kissed you. And you weren't exactly outraged by it. On the contrary, you—"

"Stop it," she whispered harshly. "I don't know what you want from me."

His gaze skimmed down her lips, and a trembling started within her. If he kissed her here and now, she didn't know what she'd do. Do what she should have done the first time he kissed her? Slap him? Scream? Or what she actually did when he'd kissed her before, get lost in the contact? That made her feel slightly sick.

But he didn't try to kiss her. Instead, he touched her unsteady lips with the tip of his finger.

"Do you need to ask me that?" he asked softly.

His touch scorched her, and she knew that even moving away from it wouldn't stop the fire. "Leave me alone," she said through gritted teeth, moving away abruptly, breaking the contact. She ducked past him and walked as quickly as she could without actually running.

"Miss?" someone asked, and Maggie looked up at Hill by the doors. "Is there something else I can do for you?"

"Could you ask someone to have my car and driver come around to the front door, please?"

"Right away, miss," Hill said, and hurried off.

Maggie stepped into the coolness of the interior. She didn't focus on the tables and bar in the cavernous main room, or the denlike atmosphere in the side rooms haloed with the smoke from expensive cigars, or the low murmur of conversation mingling with subdued piano music.

She went straight through and into the vast reception area. She crossed the worn stone floor of the two-storied area and went directly to the massive double doors that were standing open to the soft day outside.

She only stopped when she stepped out into the warm sunlight and knew that Connor wasn't behind her. She couldn't sense him, and somehow she knew if the man was anywhere close, she'd know it. She didn't look back, but headed down the sweeping entry steps to the cobbled driveway that ran through expansive formal English gardens down to the main road. The car from the Pharr house pulled up, and the driver, Marin, an elderly man in a dove gray uniform, got out and hurried around to open the back door for her. He touched the brim of his uniform cap as she slipped into the car.

It wasn't until they drove off the grounds of the club that she was able to loosen up enough to sink back into the rich leather interior. By the time they neared the Pharr estate, she could breathe with relative ease and she knew that she'd done the right thing getting away from Connor. But the lie sat bitterly on her tongue. She wasn't going to be getting married.

Poor Bill. She looked out the windows as the car swung through the gates and up the winding drive to the main house. Bill was so far out of her thought process these past few days that it was frightening, but it served the purpose of letting her know what she should have known before. She wouldn't be marrying Bill. She loved him. She probably always had, but she'd never been in love with him.

"Miss, do you need the car again today?" Marin asked as he stopped at the foot of the sprawling courtyard by the entry.

She glanced up at his reflection in the rearview

mirror and ran a hand over her face. The last thing she wanted to do was to go back into the house and be alone, knowing that even going for a swim could be dangerous for her. "I don't know. Do you have any suggestions for something to do around here?"

"There's the celebration tomorrow evening, miss."

"No, I meant for the rest of the day."

"The beach is wonderful."

"Anything else?"

"There's the movie room, with lots of copies of films, or there's the media room."

Not inside, caught between four walls where she could think. "How far from here is the cove and the caves that Sebastian Lake used?"

"We were near them at the Fortress. It's just south of there. I could drive you back there if you want. It would only take about half an hour altogether. You can get a view of the arch from the bluffs."

"Can I reach it by walking along the beach if I leave from the house?"

"Most certainly. The beach goes all the way there, and it's probably only a couple of miles to walk it."

"Are the beaches down there private property?"

"No, miss, not like north of us. But you probably can't get to the caves themselves, not unless the tide is very low. That's why it's so hard to get to the caves. You really have to take a boat. You could use the family boat, if you like, but it wouldn't be ready until later this afternoon or maybe tomorrow morning."

The area was south of here, the opposite direction from Connor's place. That would do nicely, and the walk would be a great diversion. She didn't need a boat. "I'll walk."

AS MARGARET DISAPPEARED from the terrace without a backward glance, Connor caught at his control and held on to it. She was going to be married? No, that meant nothing. A deal wasn't a deal until it was finished. He knew that.

"Can't live with them and can't live without them, eh, McKay?"

He stopped trying to figure out what had just happened—or why it seemed so damned important to him—and turned to Lars Bensonia standing by the table. The portly man dressed in a silk shirt the color of limes was the last person he wanted to talk to right then. But he stood still and said, "Excuse me?"

Bensonia glanced where Margaret had gone, then back at Connor. "Don't mean to be nosy, but I've been there, done that, and know how good a drink would probably taste to you right now. How about it?"

Connor never took any offer at face value, especially when the person offering was one of Gunner's main suppliers. No, he didn't trust this man, no more than he'd thought the wine was offered without any strings attached to it. Thank goodness Fletch had briefed him on Bensonia being here so that he wasn't surprised or unprepared for him. After everything with Margaret, he didn't need any surprises in business.

"Thanks for the wine."

"Anything else I can do for you?"

He looked at the man and found that game playing came to the forefront as naturally as breathing. He went ahead and reinforced the impression he'd been trying to give Gunner. That he was down here to relax, that he was squeezing in the negotiations at Gunner's insistence. "I don't think so. I'm just down here to relax and get away." He hoped his expression looked a bit bored. "Taking a break."

"If you're looking for fun..." His words trailed off as he motioned toward the two women he was with. It was only then that Connor noticed they were very young, and from the way he was smiling at them, they weren't his daughters. "Care to join me? There's room for one more."

The idea was distasteful at best, and sickening at worst. But Connor didn't let that show. "No, I was getting away from that sort of thing, too. You understand?"

Lars nodded. "Of course. They're driving you nuts, aren't they?" He winked slyly. "Besides, I think you've got your own fun coming sooner or later. She's a looker. She looked like she could be very good in the fun department."

Connor wasn't prepared for the sudden urge to hit the man right in his face. He'd never gone for physical tactics in his life, but that moment stunned him. "I wouldn't know. We just met."

Thankfully Fletch appeared right then. "Ready to leave, boss?"

"Yeah, more than ready," he said with a nod to Lars. "See you later."

The man knew better than to press the contact, and he left with a pat on Connor's arm and a "The offer is always open."

"So, you struck out?" Fletch asked, the faint suggestion of a smile on his face as annoying as hell right then.

"She left. Now I'm leaving." He started to turn when he spotted his lucky penny on the table where Margaret had left it. He reached for it, looked at it in his palm, then, after flipping it once in the air, he caught it and pushed it in his pocket. Then he turned and headed toward the entry.

"Back to the house, boss?"

The idea of the house right then was claustrophobic. "No, I told Gunner four, and I'm not going to be anywhere near a phone until then."

"Then where to?"

As Fletch asked, he knew. "Drop me at the boat. I'm taking it out until four."

"But you didn't have it readied," Fletch said, matching Connor's stride as they went back through the main building. "And if the vultures are circling, they'll know your boat when they see it leave the harbor."

Connor reached the front entry, ignored the smile and bright "goodbye" from the doorman and stepped out into the early afternoon. "You're right. Is there anyone at the docks you trust to keep their mouth shut?"

"Hawkins. He's safe."

"Then call him and see if he can arrange something for me to take out."

As Fletch went down the steps with Connor, he took out his cell phone, punched in a number and said, "Hawkins? Fletcher here. Can you get me a boat for today?" They reached the bottom of the steps and both men stopped by the Mercedes convertible a valet was just parking for them.

Fletch looked at Connor. "How big?" he asked.

"A cruiser, something I can handle by myself. I've got some trunks in the back of the car, so we don't have to go back to the house. Ask him if I can get it right away."

"A cruiser, right away?" Fletch nodded. "Great, we'll be right there," he said into the phone, then flipped it shut. "Done."

Connor nodded, then went around and slipped in behind the wheel of the black car. Fletch got in on the passenger side, and as he shut the door, Connor drove off. "So, where are we going on the boat?"

"We?" Connor turned onto the main road in the direction of the docks on the north shoulder of the island. "There's no *we*. Just me. I need to think, to clear my mind."

Chapter Eight

"Okay, fair enough," Fletch said. "Get some time alone. It might help you clear your head. Besides, I've got some things I need to take care of. I'll just expect you back here by four."

Connor pressed the accelerator and sped up, letting the warm air rush past him. "Thanks for finding out about Bensonia being here."

"What did he want?"

"A drink. A talk." He slowed when he neared his security gates. "He's just down here for pleasure."

"You bought that line?" Fletch asked.

"About as much as he bought mine," Connor said when he spotted the docking area ahead of them. "While you're lying around today, check on him again."

"Anything else?"

He slowed as he got near the turnoff for the storage and docking area. "Have you ever heard anyone say that I'm an egotistical, stubborn, conceited, arrogant jerk?"

Fletch hardly ever really laughed, but he did right then. Connor hit the brakes at the security gate and ignored the guard who came out of a side house. "This isn't funny."

The big man barely contained his laughter to ask, "That's what she called you?"

"Among other things," he muttered as the guard looked into the car, then nodded and opened the gates for him.

"That's why she walked out on you?"

"No, she's going to be married," he said as he drove slowly through the double gates and onto a graveled parking area to the left of the docking sites.

"Well, that changes things, don't you think?"

He turned off the car and glanced at Fletch, who couldn't quite lose the humor on his face. "Maybe, maybe not. Going to be married isn't being married."

"Okay. If you can raise that much passion in her, for her to call you egotistical, arrogant, stubborn, conceited and a jerk, maybe you will have a chance."

Fletch got out, then reached in the back of the car for his duffel bag. Connor was already standing by the car when the big man slipped in behind the wheel and started the engine. As he put it in reverse, he said, "Oh, by the way, I've never heard anyone call you a jerk, if that helps." He flashed a grin, then backed out and left.

As Connor glared at the car leaving through the gates, he realized what Fletch had said. Passionate? Margaret? Hell, yes, she was very passionate. He'd felt that passion, and as he spotted Hawkins by a sleek-looking cruiser halfway down the floating dock, he knew with certainty that he'd never get enough of her passion.

MAGGIE WALKED SOUTH on the beach for what seemed forever, past a scattering of homes high on the bluffs above her, along a thin ribbon of silky sand. The sun was warm through the lacy coverup she was wearing over her white halter top and cutoff jeans shorts. The sand felt silky under her bare feet, and when she passed the Fortress high above her on the rocks, she didn't look up.

She kept going, heading south until the Fortress was behind her, and she spotted a massive jutting of the bluff out into the ocean, its sides smoothed from water and wind over the years. The huge rocks at the bottom, half in the water, looked as if they would block her from going any farther.

But as she got closer, she could see the rocks were climbable, almost forming a lip along the base of the jutting section. Carefully, she scrambled up onto the lower rocks, got her footing and managed to use the larger rocks to her right for support as she climbed around the bottom along a twenty-foot stretch that fell away into the water.

As she rounded the corner, she stopped on a smooth rock and faced something that almost took her breath away with its natural beauty. It was the arch. The wall cut back, and she found herself looking at a natural bridge from one side of the stone bluff to the other, sweeping from side to side at least forty feet above deep turquoise waters.

She neared the side of the arch and had to wade into the water to go around the last barrier until she finally spotted the famous cove. It was as awesome as the arch, an almost perfect circle of space, maybe half a mile across. The water was so true blue that it shimmered, and swaying palms framed it, gently ruffled by a soft breeze off the ocean. The cry of seabirds echoed off the stone walls where she could see a series of pockmarks at the far back of the sheltered area.

She made her way up onto a narrow beach of pressed sand that seemed oddly hard and embedded with the ridges of tide erosion. The peace was almost palpable in the place, and Maggie could feel the tension in her dissolving. She looked around, then impulsively shrugged out of her cover-up, tossed it on the sand and waded out into the water. She kept going until the water lapped at the bottom of her shorts, then she dove into the water.

Her hand stung slightly from the saltwater under the smaller bandage, but that was soon forgotten as she stroked down into the blueness. She could see the rock-scattered bottom as it fell away radically into deep shadows where fish skittered past as if she didn't exist. Marin had been right about bringing a boat. The cove could have easily handled a craft that could be anchored on the still waters.

She swam leisurely, out farther, and when she looked around, she was closer to the arch than the back shoreline. She dove under again, stroked back away from the arch, and this time when she surfaced, she was nearing the back beach. She shook her head as she treaded water, then realized there was something different. A new sound. A droning noise that hadn't been there before.

As she glanced in the direction of the arched entrance to the cove, she caught a flash of something. The next thing she knew, a boat was there, a sleek vessel, maybe twenty or thirty feet long, gleaming white in the sunlight, with a deep blue stripe at the water line. It was gliding past the opening. Then it was gone out of sight, and the sound died out with it.

Maggie turned and stroked toward the back beach, and by the time she got to shore, she felt pleasantly tired. The sand was firm here, too, cut by the ribbons that showed the tide lines, and the warmth of the sun was wonderful. Perfect, she thought as she looked ahead over the thin strip of beach at the granite walls of the bluffs. Some tall palms pressed against the rough surface, casting short shadows from the early afternoon sun near a crude opening in the bluff.

She went a bit closer, noting that the opening was about twelve feet tall and eight across, with sand washed up to the threshold, making a low barrier there. This had to be the cave Sebastian Lake used to trap his prey. She was about to step into it to look inside, when she heard that droning sound again. But this time it was coming closer. She turned just as the boat she'd seen before skimmed under the granite arch and into the calm waters of the cove. It slowed, stopped, then as the engine died, she caught sight of someone on the deck.

Shading her eyes from the glare of the sun with one hand, she could make out someone near the side of the boat. A man. Dark hair. Then he was climbing onto the side rail, standing straight in the clear light, and she recognized Connor. In the next heartbeat, she realized that he looked very naked.

One minute he was standing on the rail at the front of the boat, the next he had dived cleanly into the deep blue of the waters of the cove. When he broke the surface with a slight splash, all of her peace was gone. She felt her heart hit her ribs uncomfortably.

Damn it all, he never left her alone. He always turned up, and she hated the part of her that felt pleasure at the sight of him. That part that felt fire at the idea of him naked in the water. But the other part, the rational part of her being, knew what true foolishness could be.

The foolishness that drove her to hold her breath until he broke the surface. The foolishness of thinking she had any right to feel a sense of anticipation as he shook his head to clear the water. The foolishness of knowing that if she had any right to be here with him, she wouldn't run from him at all.

But she couldn't be here with him. She couldn't be close to him again. Never.

She saw him glance in her direction, then start to stroke toward her through the water. For what seemed an eternity, she was frozen to the spot, then as he neared the shore, she knew that no matter what, she wasn't going to stand here and watch him come out of the water. No, that was something she wouldn't do again. Ever.

She looked for escape but knew that there was no way she could get to the arch before he could catch her. Swimming through the arch was out of the question, and her only option was the cave. She turned to it and realized that she only had to cross about twenty feet of hard sand to get to it.

When she heard the splashing of his swim strokes, she looked back to find Connor almost to the shore. He was just starting to stand, to get out of the water. He was waist-deep in the water now, his face etched by the bright sunlight, and for a moment she could have sworn he was as shocked to see her there as she was to see him. Then the expression was gone, and a smile that was as blinding as the sun, replaced it. Maggie felt her legs weaken and her breathing tighten. She turned away from the sight of him.

"Margaret?" he called, his voice coming to her on the warm air, echoing off the granite walls around her. But she didn't look back as she headed across the sand for the cave.

Connor rose out of the water at the same time Margaret turned and rushed away from him. Shock and pleasure were equally mixed in him. He blessed fate, or whatever perverse system had brought him here and brought her here. He wasn't going to question it. No more than he questioned that edge of anger he felt when he realized she was running away from him again.

He was on the beach going after her, getting closer to her in her wet denim shorts and skimpy halter top. He got so close to her partially naked back that he could see the smooth skin, the way her wet hair clung to her bare shoulders, the movement of her hips, the stride of her long legs. Damn it, he wasn't just going after her, he was almost running, and he forced himself to stop as she reached the entrance to the cave.

"Margaret, what in the hell is going on with you?" he called out, his voice echoing off the walls around them.

She stopped abruptly, framed against a strange dimness inside the cave, a murky type of light that blurred the defining lines of her body. But he didn't miss the tension in her stance, or the way she deliberately didn't turn back to him.

She reached out and touched the eroded side wall of the entrance, her fingers long and elegant—and ringless—against the rough stone.

"What are you doing here?" she asked without turning.

Being a fool, he thought, but instead used sarcasm as a defense. "Just being an egotistical, stubborn, conceited, arrogant jerk, I guess."

She didn't turn even then, but he could see her take a slightly shaky breath. "You're doing a good job of it," she muttered in a voice that faintly echoed back from the cave in front of her.

"Ah, being put down in stereo," he said wryly. "How unique. At least look at me while you're doing it."

He heard her take a sharp breath, then she turned, actually spun around toward him, her hair moving and the water caught in it spraying coolly over his skin. Her eyes flicked over him, then she exhaled in a rush. "I thought you…you were…"

"I was what?" he asked, not understanding her look of relief now.

She waved one hand vaguely. "I thought you didn't have any…" She bit her lip as her eyes flicked to his beige swim trunks, then back to his face. "From a distance it looked as if—"

He understood and would have laughed if she hadn't looked so damned serious and if high color hadn't invaded her cheeks. "You thought I was naked?" He loved the way she blushed, truly a unique gift in his circles. "No, not this time. Only at night when I think I'm alone."

She stood very still, then asked abruptly, "What are you doing here?"

Good question, he thought, but shrugged. "You mentioned this place and I had the boat." That sounded so lame, but it was the truth. She'd mentioned Sebastian Lake's cave and it had stuck with him for some reason. "I've never even been near here before and I was curious about the cove." He narrowed his eyes on her. "How about you?"

He didn't miss the way her tongue touched her pale pink lips. "I...I'm here to explore the caves and have some time to myself...alone."

He could feel that frustration rising in him as he realized that something he hated was happening with her. He hated not being able to figure out someone. He prided himself on being good at that very thing, yet with Margaret, he always felt as if he was one step behind and in the dark. Although, being in the dark with her sounded appealing. Way too appealing when she seemed so bent on cutting him dead.

He heard himself saying something he hadn't planned on asking. "I was wondering who you're going to marry."

She blinked at him. "Why?"

"I probably know him."

"No, you don't," she said quickly.

"Okay, then tell me what he does."

"Banking."

"International?"

"I don't know. Just banking." She swiped at her damp curls, brushing them back from her face, a slightly vulnerable action that he didn't quite understand. "He's not one to talk about his business."

"I know a lot of bankers. Or is he in investments?"

"I really don't know," she said with a touch of exasperation. "Now, I—"

"Martin Rossling."

"Who?"

"Martin Rossling. Is that who you're getting engaged to?" If he knew his competition, maybe he could figure this all out.

"No, of course not."

"You said he was in banking—"

"William Rome," she said on a sigh that was tinged with impatience. "His name is William Rome. And I'm sure you don't know him."

He'd never heard of him. "You're right, I don't."

She sighed heavily. "Now, can I go?"

He tried to think, but her closeness made sensible thought all but impossible. There was her physical beauty, that was obvious, but his fascination went beyond that, to a place he couldn't begin to define. That disturbed him more than anything. He loved control, and with Margaret he had none.

She nibbled impatiently on her bottom lip, and that was totally distracting, too. Especially when he could almost taste her essence on his tongue.

"You can't go in the caves," he said, the words coming out abruptly.

She frowned slightly. "Of course I can. I just have to turn and go inside."

"No, I meant, you shouldn't go in there."

"Why?"

"No one around here goes in there. It's too dangerous." He remembered hearing that somewhere, then he added logically, "Besides, you don't have a light."

"I don't need one. There are airholes that come down from the surface all through the tunnel system. They let in some light, making something like perpetual dusk. At least that's how it was described in one of the books. So, I don't need a light."

"It's too dangerous, with or without a light."

The frown deepened, drawing a fine line between her deep blue eyes. "Dangerous?"

"Yes, it fills up at high tide, that's how old Sebastian captured his prey."

"I thought you didn't know anything about Lake?" she said, her head cocking a bit to one side as she studied him with those blue eyes.

"I didn't, not until you filled me in, then the man I got the boat from told me a bunch of things while he was getting it ready for me. He talked my ear off about the guy. And something else about your Sebastian Lake."

"He's not *my* Sebastian Lake," she said firmly.

"Okay, but I found out he wasn't the tough guy they say he was. He was a devout coward, who ambushed his prey and never once had a battle on water. He used those caves, lured his enemies into them just before high tide, cut them off when it flooded, then ambushed them when they couldn't get out."

"Your boat man was right. That's exactly what he did," she said. "But it's not high tide now, and it won't be high enough to flood for hours. And there's no pirate in there waiting to ambush me."

He was hitting a brick wall with her, and he hated the feeling. He'd had enough, and his words held a biting sarcasm that he hadn't intended to use. "You've got such an attitude that if old Sebastian ambushed you, you could freeze him out. You'll be safe."

He saw a flash of something in her eyes that could have been pain from his words, but she didn't strike back at him. She quietly turned away from him, and the next thing he knew, she was gone, disappearing into the caves.

He'd never batted an eye at cutting down anyone with words in business. That was part of his arsenal when he needed it. But the look he saw in Margaret's eyes because of what he'd said wouldn't leave him. He turned from the cave entrance and crossed to the water's edge, but he didn't swim out to the boat anchored in the cove.

He stood there, the water swirling around his ankles while he dealt with an odd emotion for him. Remorse. God, he'd so seldom felt that that he had trouble even identifying it, and when he did, it just added to his confusion. Damn it, he hated what was going on. He hated what he'd just done. He hated a man called William Rome, and he hated the fact that he had made everything worse than it had been when she'd walked out on him at the Fortress. But most of all, he hated losing control.

Then he realized there was one thing he could control, their last contact, and it wasn't going to be what had just happened. He turned and went back to the cave's opening. He'd apologize to her, then leave her to explore the caves if she wanted to. But he wouldn't leave with this bitter taste in his mouth.

He stepped into the dusky shadows, where the air took on a damp chill overlaid with a certain mustiness of the sea. He could feel the cool stones of the floor under his feet, stones worn smooth by the tides that flooded over them.

He waited a moment for his eyes to adjust, then he went farther into the tunnel. It sloped downward, framed by rough walls and a ceiling that was about three feet over his head. He was startled when he

took a step and realized he'd stepped into cold, an-
kle-deep water. He could barely make out a darker
shadow that was water stretching out in front of him
for about ten feet.

Margaret had to have gone this way, so it couldn't
be too deep. He carefully waded through the shallow
water, then out onto more smooth stone sloping up.
He kept going, wondering just how far Margaret
would go before she turned and came back. With
each step he took, he thought she'd be there, coming
back toward him, and he found himself literally tensing as he waited to face her again.

He'd apologize. He'd make amends, then he'd
leave and let her have her life. He followed the path
through twists and turns, always upward, then suddenly, he emerged into a chamber, a wide space with
a ceiling that soared upward into dusky shadows and
blurred darkness. There was no exit that he could see,
yet Margaret wasn't there.

He stopped in the middle of the space. There
hadn't been any side tunnels, any offshoots where
she could have gone, but he was alone in the cavern.
That wasn't possible. It hadn't been an illusion, Margaret at the opening to the cave, them talking, the
way he'd hurt her. No, that had been real, very real.
He hadn't imagined it.

She had to be here. Somewhere. He stood in the
center of the space and shouted out to her. "Margaret?" His voice bounced back at him from every
nook and cranny, over and over again.

The echo hadn't faded completely before there
was another sound, a deafening crash mingled with
a piercing scream. The noises echoed over him and
around him, then there was silence, a silence almost
as horrible as the scream had been a heartbeat before.

Chapter Nine

"Margaret?" Connor yelled, his voice reverberating everywhere. God, he could feel a pain in his chest and he could barely breathe. He cupped his hands to his mouth and yelled again. "Margaret?"

Nothing but his own voice echoing around him. He looked at the space above him, and in the blurred dimness, he could see what looked like crude steps cut in the granite side wall that led up to deep shadows halfway up the wall. He hurried to them but froze when he heard something.

Margaret. "I'm here." He could barely make out her weak voice carrying in the dusky shadows over him.

"Where's here?" he called as he got to the steps and started up toward her voice.

"I don't know." Her voice reverberated all around him. "Somewhere down the second tunnel. The high one."

He stepped up onto a deeply cut platform and saw another opening that seemed to glow faintly in the deep shadows. He hurried across to it. "What was all that noise?"

"It was me falling."

"Falling? Are you okay?" he asked, a bit surprised by the way her words made his chest clench uncomfortably.

"I think so," she replied, her voice drifting to him along the winding passageway. "I should have known it was there, but I wasn't looking."

"Keep talking so I can find you," he called to her into what looked like another part of the tunnel system. "And tell me what you should have known was there and how you fell."

"I should have remembered about the trap. I should have known. I just read about it, for heaven's sake." Her voice didn't sound weak now or as if she was hurt, but just plain angry. His chest eased as he hurried forward and listened to her words all around him.

"Either age just rotted everything, or Sebastian had a trap set in case any of the men got away and tried to make a break this way."

"A trap?" he asked as he got to a spot in the tunnel where it was barely high enough for him to stand up straight.

"I forget what it's called, but you remember the stories where a hunter traps a bear by digging a hole, then makes it look like it was safe ground by putting tree limbs and leaves over it to hide it?"

"You fell in a hole?"

"You've got it," she said, not shouting now, but her voice coming clearly to him on several echoes. "And there's no way out, at least not that I can find."

"How deep is it?"

"I don't know. Maybe eight feet or so, and it's

dark as night down here. I can't see a thing, except a bit of light at the top.''

He hurried toward her voice. ''Are you sure you aren't hurt?''

''I don't think so.'' There was a pause, then a muffled ''Oh, darn!''

''What is it?'' he demanded as he stumbled trying to get to her faster.

''Something fell on my head,'' she cried, and he could tell he was getting much closer.

''Quit moving around. Stand still until I can get there,'' he called.

''Stop!'' she yelled suddenly. ''You're close. Be careful.''

He stopped in his tracks as he rounded a corner to find air that was filled with drifting dust. Less than five feet in front of him was a yawning black hole where the path should have been, so far across that he couldn't see the other side.

He moved cautiously forward, then, feeling the rocks under his feet shift slightly, he stopped. ''Margaret, are you down there?''

''Yes, I'm here. I can see you sort of. You're right above me.''

He looked into the hole, but the light the airholes provided above didn't touch the space below him. He dropped to his haunches and peered into the blackness, but he couldn't see her at all. ''It's about eight feet deep?''

''I think so. I can't reach the top.''

She was closer, he could tell, and he suddenly wanted nothing more than just to be able to see her, touch her and make sure she was okay.

''It's all rocks and sand, and I can't climb them.

They keep moving under my feet. Just go and get someone, and I'll wait here. I'm not going anywhere.'' He was shocked when she actually chuckled at that. ''That's the truth.''

He couldn't smile, and the idea of leaving her here while he went for help didn't sit well with him. But he had no options. Until he moved. Then any options he might have had were taken from him. He felt the earth give beneath his foot, then he was falling down into the darkness.

He heard Margaret yell at the same time he landed in, thankfully, forgiving silt and sand. For a long moment he lay there, then she touched him. Margaret's hand was on his side, then his arm, her fingers clutching his upper arm so tightly it blocked out any lingering pain from his fall. ''Oh God, no!'' she cried in a shaky voice. ''Oh, no, no.''

He knew the only thing hurt was his pride, but he didn't move for a moment longer. The feeling of Margaret's hands on him, moving urgently upward to touch his throat, then his chin, was just too damn good to stop it. Then her fingers touched his lips, and he could feel the trembling in them. Enough, he thought, and covered her hand with his.

She started at the contact, jerking back, breaking the contact, leaving a horribly empty feeling in its place. Any pleasure was gone, and he rolled onto his side. ''That first step is murder,'' he said, grasping at humor that fell just about as flatly as he'd fallen moments ago.

''You're okay?'' The whispered voice was close, so close, but there was no more gentle touch to soothe his wounded soul.

He pushed up until he was standing in the silty

sand and rocks, one hand braced on the rough side of the cave-in. "Sure, I'm okay." He swiped at the sand that clung to his skin with his other hand. "Here I was worried about leaving you here at the mercy of old Sebastian's ghost, and now we're both trapped."

"We're safe from Sebastian Lake, ghost or not," she said in that soft voice that seemed to draw at every nerve in his body. "Didn't you say I could freeze him out?"

"Touché," he said as he steadied himself for a moment before he turned in the darkness toward the sound of her voice. He wasn't prepared to literally feel Margaret's presence so close to him at that moment. He knew if he reached out, he'd be touching her the way she'd touched him moments ago. Actually, he ached to touch her, to have that connection with her again in the darkness, to make sure she was okay, too. No, that wasn't entirely true. He wanted to touch her for more reasons than just checking on her welfare.

"You were right. It's dark as night down here." But that wasn't entirely true, either. As his eyes adjusted a bit more, he could vaguely make her out, a deeper shadow in the darkness. "Are you sure you're not hurt?"

"I'm *not* hurt. I just sort of tumbled down. I think a rock fell on my head when I was trying to climb out before, but that's it."

He took his chances and put his hand out in front of him. He felt her instantly, soft and warm, her shoulder, he thought, and he also felt the way she jerked at the sudden contact. "Where did it hit you?" he asked, moving a bit closer.

She was very still under his hand now, then, without warning, her hand was on his. He literally held his breath as she lifted his hand, guiding it up until he was touching her face at her hairline near her temple. The tips of his fingers brushed a large swelling, then her hand left his. Undaunted, he kept his hand in place and gingerly fingered the swelling, but he couldn't feel any broken skin.

"A real goose egg," he said, and realized that he'd finally taken a breath.

She drew back from his touch, until there was nothing there for him. Just darkness, and the taunting knowledge that all he had to do was put out his hand and he could touch her. But he didn't. Instead, he drew back a bit and looked overhead. It was ten feet up at least, and the walls seemed to be comprised of nothing but loose rocks and silt—not the ideal situation for climbing.

"We'll never be able to climb back up there," she said to him through the darkness, as if she'd read his mind. "We're trapped. You shouldn't have gotten so close."

"'Should have's' don't count," he muttered. "Not in business, and they sure as hell don't count in a situation like this. It wouldn't do any good to start saying you should have been watching more carefully for something like this. After all, it's a pirate's cave, a guy who pillaged and plundered and, obviously, didn't play fair. Or, you should have at least believed me when I told you it was dangerous in here."

"You were talking about the tide filling the other tunnel, and if you hadn't yelled at me, I would have been looking for this sort of thing, or at least paying attention.''

''I yelled at you?''

''You shouted, and do you know how that echoed in this place?''

''I called out to you. I got in that room back there and didn't see the ledge, and you were nowhere around. I thought you'd disappeared into thin air.''

''Sure, the same way I freeze out pirates.''

He acted on impulse then, reaching out into the darkness to find her. She was there, startled by his touch, and when she would have moved back from him, he didn't let her. He gripped her upper arm and held her where she was, lightly but surely. ''I shouldn't have said that.''

''Damn straight you shouldn't have. You don't even know me.''

He didn't, but why did he feel as if he'd known her all of his life? Or maybe it was more that he'd been looking for her all of his life. No, that was ridiculous. He hadn't even known she existed until that moment when he'd found her on the beach. He drew his hand back, balling it into a fist at his side. ''I'm sorry,'' he said, words that didn't come easily for him. ''I regret saying that. I didn't mean it.''

Maggie moved back from Connor, needing desperately to find some distance when little existed in the black hole. She rubbed at her arm where he'd touched her, but it didn't do a thing to take that feeling away from her. It felt as if he'd branded her, and it would never go away. She bit her lip hard, then took a breath. ''You don't need to apologize. Just get us out of here.''

She sensed him move and she took a step back to

avoid any more contact. But he brushed past her, his essence remaining in the air that he stirred as he moved about the hole. "This side looks better," he said from behind her, his voice slightly muffled.

There was the sound of rocks falling, a strange tinkling sound, then there was silence, touched only by the sound of Connor breathing.

She turned and stood very still, trying to see what he was doing, but the shadows were too thick. "Can we get out?" she finally asked when she couldn't stand the silence any longer.

She almost jumped out of her skin when Connor spoke from right in front of her. "Yes, we can do this." The darkness hid him, and she hated that. She hated not being able to see his eyes in order to figure out what was going on. Then she amended that. No, sometimes the darkness was better. Meeting his gaze made everything so crazy. She took another step back.

"Do what?" she managed to ask.

"Get out of here. The far side's firmer, as if it's been caved in for a while and settled. If we're careful, we can climb up and over the edge."

"Are you sure?"

"No written guarantee, but I think so. The wall slopes out a bit, which should make climbing easier." He exhaled harshly in the shadows. "I think I'll take your suggestion. I'll get out, go for help, then come back for you."

If he could get out, she could get out, and she wasn't about to stay down here by herself, no matter what she'd told him earlier. "Oh, no you don't. I'm going, too."

"I thought you said—"

"That was when you were up there and I was down here. If you can get out, I can get out."

"You aren't dizzy or faint at all?" he asked.

"No, I'm okay. Let's just get out of here."

"Okay, if you say so," he said, and she sensed him moving again. "I should do the gentlemanly thing and let you go first, but I don't think that'll work here. I'll go first and test the climb. When I make it out, I'll help you up." The sound of rocks falling echoed in the hole from across the space.

"I can go out first," she said quickly.

"No, you can't. I'm going to do it."

She wanted to argue, but bit her lip as she moved toward his voice. Instead, she asked, "What are you doing now?"

"Climbing." His voice came from a bit higher in the space now.

"Climbing?"

"Hand over hand," he said in a tight voice. "And with great difficulty." He was higher now, and she knew a moment of complete horror when she could feel the distance between them growing.

"Oh, no you don't," she said, scrambling after him, reaching out to find the far side of the hole. "I'm not staying down here by myself." She couldn't quite kill the panic in her voice as she saw a blur at the top of the hole. He was almost out, and she scrambled after him. "I'm coming."

Next time she looked up, he was at the top, looking down at her. "It's pretty solid up here, but take it easy. Make sure you've got good footing before you push."

"Sure," she said, and started up, grabbing at any handhold she could find and pushing with her feet.

She grasped the roughness of the wall, amazed that she was actually able to climb and pull herself farther and farther up.

''Here, take my hand,'' Connor said from above her, and when she looked up, she was surprised to see she was almost to the top.

She steadied herself, then reached blindly above her. All at once, Connor had her. His hand was strong and warm around hers, and his strength was helping her make the last part of the journey. Then she was up at the top of the hole, and with one single pull, Connor had her out on the rocky path with him.

Her impetus sent her reeling forward, right into him, knocking him back and her with him. They tangled together on the ground, then she realized that they weren't tangled at all. He was holding her, and she was lying across his chest, his heartbeat against her cheek.

Right then she knew what paradise really was. Not the island, not the life-style, or lunch at a fabulous club, but being held like this by this man. That aching truth burned through her, and she couldn't move.

Then Connor was easing her back, and she was over him, looking down at him, her hair falling around her face. And she could see him, his features blurred, but that didn't stop a surge of pleasure at just being able to see him at all. She loved the sight of him.

It was as simple as that.

And that terrible.

Love. God help her, but she knew right then that she could love this man with a singleness of heart that she'd never known before. The thought stunned her. Love? Not that. She had to stop it now. Someway, somehow. But she didn't know how to do it. Except to get away from him.

"Thanks," she breathed, and rolled away from him to scramble to her feet. She felt a surge of light-headedness that she doubted had anything to do with the blow to her head, and everything to do with Connor as she pressed a hand to the wall to steady herself for a moment.

Then he was there, standing in front of her, touching her gently, brushing her hair back from her face. She was very still, absorbing the feeling of his hand, as light as a feather on her skin. "You really do have a huge bump there," he said, gingerly touching the soreness by her temple.

She trembled, and his hand shifted to cup her chin warmly. "Hey, kid, it's okay. We made it. We're out of there," he said, then as if it were the most natural thing in the world, he dipped his head and his lips touched hers. There was no passion in the contact, just reassurance, a way of saying he was there, and she let it sink into her soul. Before she rejected the whole thing.

She moved away slowly, breaking the torturous contact and turning away from him as she hugged her arms tightly around herself. "I can't believe this all happened," she said.

"It's all my fault," he said from behind her.

"No, it's not. I shouldn't have said that." She turned, thankful now that he was a bit farther away from her and that the dimness hid his eyes. "You yelled, but I wasn't looking."

"Okay, okay, tell you what? We'll call it even. Deal?"

She could tell he was holding out his hand to her,

but she didn't take it. Instead, she nodded. "Yes, that's a deal," she whispered. "Now, let's go back and get out of here. I think I'm starting to develop claustrophobia."

He turned, then stopped. "Oh, damn."

"What's wrong now?" she asked.

"We're on the wrong side," he said. "We climbed out on the far side of the cave-in, not where you fell in. We can't get back unless we go back in the hole and try to climb out on the other end. And we probably couldn't even get out on the other side with the way the debris is piled. We're stuck."

"Wrong."

He turned to her. "What?"

"We can get out going this way." She motioned in the opposite direction. "It goes up and comes out somewhere under the original castle. At least that's what the books hinted at. Something about two exits. I mean, they weren't specific, but it's a given that Lake had more than one way to trap people and get out himself."

"Under the original castle, as in under the ground?"

"No, as in something like dungeons, rooms that Lake would have kept his prisoners in until he figured out just how they'd die."

"Which was?"

"Hanging, drawing and quartering or the ever-popular walking the plank." She motioned with her arms. "This way has to go up."

"You must have a photographic memory."

"I just remember things," she said.

"Thank goodness. Now, if you feel up to walking, just lead the way. I'll follow you anywhere."

Even if she didn't feel up to it, she was going to start walking. She didn't want to be down here with Connor any longer. "Okay, let's go."

She turned and started off, up the passageway, leaving the gaping hole behind them. Connor was right behind her, the sensation of him at her back ever constant, and she hurried even more.

"So, there was method in old Lake's madness? He made his own escape route," Connor said.

"No, he made his own entry to the caves so he could be in here when the others got trapped, and so he could get out just as easily. He wasn't a stupid man, that's for sure. Bloodthirsty, but not stupid."

As she walked, her legs began to feel a bit rubbery, and she slowed her pace a bit as they climbed farther. Then she rounded a corner and stopped dead in her tracks. Connor ran into her, grabbing her shoulders to keep them both on their feet, then his breath was at her ear. "Don't tell me there's another hole?"

Maggie stared into the shadows, at the place where the tunnel split into two routes, each going in diametrically opposite directions. "No, a fork in the road, so to speak."

Connor was up beside her now, his shoulder against hers, and she didn't move away from the contact. She didn't have the energy to do anything more than stare at the two paths right then.

"Okay, Margaret, you're the expert on this. Which way do we go?"

"I don't know. What I read wasn't that specific. It just described the way Lake trapped the men, and how he could get out. It never mentioned a damned fork."

"Well, should we flip a coin to see which way to go?"

"Be serious," she said with a frustrated sigh.

He leaned closer to her, his lips near her ear. "I *am* serious. When you don't have a clue about something, tossing a coin is as good a thing as any to help make a decision. I've done it before with my lucky penny, and nine times out of ten, it works."

She glanced at him beside her, the closeness unsettling. "Then flip your penny."

Despite the shadows, she could almost see the smile. "Sorry, it's in my other pants. This is your call. Which way?"

"I don't know. How can I choose?"

"Go with your gut instinct. Which way feels right?"

The only thing she "felt" right about was him being so close to her. That just showed how dependable her feelings were right then. She moved ahead and away from him, up to the point where the passage split. This close, she could tell the one on the right was higher and larger, and the one on the left was lower-ceilinged and seemed to get even lower as it went back.

"To the right," she said, pointing to it. "That way."

He was by her side, not moving. "Nice. You sound as if you know what you're talking about."

"No, I'm just invariably logical. Lake was a tall man, almost six foot, and in those days that was considered very tall." She pointed to the left path. "Look how low that ceiling is in there. Lake couldn't have walked in there very easily, much less fought in there, if he had to."

He startled her by touching her bare shoulder, laying his hand there. "Good point. Very logical. Let's get going."

She moved away from him, vaguely disoriented for a moment when he took his hand off her shoulder. Then the foolish feeling was gone and she moved as quickly as she could into the right passage.

It took her a moment to realize that the walls of the cave were now smoother, the ceiling was straight across and the light was failing. The shadows were inky in this part, and just when she began to think she couldn't see enough to go on, she reached a dead end. There was a solid barrier in front of her. When she reached out to touch it, she found it was rough wood, damp and gritty.

"What is it?" Connor asked, but didn't wait for an answer before he reached over her shoulder and touched the wood. "A door?"

"It could be," she said. "But it's so dark, it's hard to tell."

He moved around her, his body brushing against hers as he went in front of her, and she could sense him touching the wood. Then she heard a low, spooky creaking sound. "A door, and it's open. We're free."

The creaking echoed in the tunnel, then there was the sound of the door softly thudding against an inner wall. But the darkness was still black as ink, and Maggie stayed where she was. Then she heard Connor move, and she could sense he was gone, that he'd entered the place beyond the door.

"There's got to be something," he said softly as he moved farther from her, then, without warning, there was light.

It was low, a dull glow, but seemed almost brilliant after the darkness she'd been in. As she stepped toward the light, she saw Connor in front of her, and the sight of him, after being led by his voice and his shadow, seemed overwhelming.

Tall and lean in his skimpy swim trunks, he was looking at her, his hair skimmed back from his face, and there was a smile on that face that riveted her to the spot. "No dungeons," he said on a chuckle. "But a fully stocked wine cellar." With a small high window to provide light.

She stared at him, and knew that the thoughts she'd had earlier in the dark were a reality. She could love him. Damn it, she could really love him. That very thought made her brace herself before she moved toward him.

Connor watched Margaret come out of the shadows toward him, and the lurch in his chest made his smile falter. All of his resolve to apologize, then get the hell out of her life, were shattered in that moment. She came into the light as the door behind her swung shut with a creak that startled her for a moment. Then she was carefully moving toward him. Her hair was drying into a halo of curls, and her skimpy shorts and halter top barely covered the curves and angles of the body that he'd felt with his hands before.

He had to look away when his body began to respond in a very obvious way to the image before him. He turned toward the cellar, a large space filled with row upon row of heavy wooden frames that held dusty bottles of wine. The walls were stone, the floor was laid with worn tiles, and he could see a door set in a stone arch directly across from the access to the caves.

"So, this is all part of Lake's old place?" he asked, partly to fill the emptiness and also to take his mind off Margaret as he crossed to the door.

"I'm sure it wasn't a wine cellar when Lake was around this place, but it's probably part of the Fortress, at least on the grounds of the place."

"A distant place on the grounds, if this dust is any indication of activity down here. It doesn't look as if anyone's been in here for a very long time."

"If it's part of the club, why wouldn't anyone be down here...." He saw her glance around as her voice trailed off. Then she was looking at him. "All this wine wouldn't just be forgotten."

He needed out of here, and the door was so close. He headed for it. "I'm sure it's not, but this could be more of a storage cellar than an active wine cellar. Put wine here, let it age naturally." He shrugged, his interest in wine right then almost nonexistent as he got to the door. "Either way, it's been closed up for a while."

He grasped the metal hasp and pulled, but nothing happened. He pulled harder, but there was no movement at all. "Locked," he said, hitting the barrier with his closed fist. "Hello!" he yelled, but nothing happened. "Hey, is anyone out there?" Nothing.

He stood very still, then something in him clicked into line as he realized what he was doing. He was trapped in a wine cellar with Margaret. He had her all to himself, and he was hitting the door and screaming to be rescued. That didn't make sense at all. He had her alone, time to talk and get to know her even better. A time for him, with no William Rome around. He was a man who always took advantage of the situation, no matter how negative it seemed. And this wasn't negative. Not at all.

Chapter Ten

Connor turned and tried to act annoyed. "Damn it, no one's out there."

She was still across the space, down the center aisle near the closed door they'd come in through. Hugging her arms around herself, she seemed very vulnerable at that moment, then a frown tugged at her features. Connor experienced a wave of protectiveness right then that was only matched by what he'd felt when she'd cut her hand. He wanted to protect this woman from every bad thing in the world, and he wanted to be the one to make her smile.

"We have to get out," she said, then turned and was grasping the metal hasp of the back door. He stood very still as she tugged on the door, but it didn't move. "Oh, great, just great," she muttered. "It's stuck."

"We can't go back that way," he said without crossing to pull on the door for her. "Remember the hole?"

She turned to him, her features slightly blurred, but he could see the set of her jaw. "Remember the branch in the tunnel?" she retorted.

"Remember how shallow the ceiling was? We'd probably get stuck in it."

"Maybe, but..." She bit her full bottom lip. "Open this door, and I'll go and look for myself."

He hated logic when it interfered with what he wanted, but he crossed to where she stood, not missing the way she moved back to avoid any contact with him. He grasped the handle and pulled, not as hard as he probably should have, but hard enough to realize that the door had become securely wedged shut after they'd entered the wine cellar. He pulled harder. He didn't have to lie when he looked at Margaret. "It won't budge."

"Someone has to be close by. Surely they'll hear us."

Silently, he went back to the other door, hit it with his fist. "Hello! Hello!" Then he turned to Margaret, who hadn't moved from the spot where he'd left her. "Sorry, no one's out there right now."

She came toward him, avoiding the cases of wine that had been piled on the end of the nearest rack. "Someone has to be there. That shadow of yours should be popping up any time."

"Shadow?" he asked, standing straighter.

"Fletch. He's always right behind you. He'll be looking for you, won't he?" She stopped a few feet from him, but he could have sworn that the air grew warmer from her closeness. "If he finds your boat abandoned, he'll probably call out the marines."

He chuckled softly at that image. "He'll look, but he'll be discreet. He knows better than to draw too much attention to me."

"What if he comes in the cave and falls in the hole?"

"Fletch? Naw, he'd never fall in a hole. He knows everything that's going on everywhere. Trust me. He'll be fine. Who's going to be looking for you? William Rome?"

She shivered involuntarily, deepening that need in him to make things better for her. "He's not here," she said softly.

"He's not coming down for the vacation?"

"No, he's busy with work." She turned from him and seemed to be looking at the wine racks. "They'll need wine sooner or later, won't they?"

"Not from this place," he said. "Not unless Lars Bensonia demands a bottle that they haven't put in the active cellar." She looked back at him, and he almost reconsidered his decision to take advantage of their isolation. She almost looked afraid. "Listen, we're in a wine cellar, an inactive one, but we're probably right beside or below the club, and, as you said, sooner or later someone's going to come down to get some very expensive wine. Things could be worse."

"Could they?" she whispered.

When she spoke, something in him snapped. She was afraid of him. Damn it, he didn't understand it, and it drove him to move toward her. He got within inches of her and said, "Okay, we're locked in, and we aren't going anywhere. So let's take advantage of it." Her eyes widened, but he didn't stop. "We've got plenty of time for you to tell me what I ever did for you to be so angry at me and so afraid of me. You said I'm stubborn, and damn it, I am. So, explain it to me so I understand. You owe me that."

Maggie had thought she'd started to feel claustrophobic in the caves, but right then she knew what real claustrophobia was. She knew what it meant not to be able to breathe and feel panic just one step away. Connor had neatly trapped her between the wine racks and himself. And she wasn't going to touch him to get around him.

She grabbed at anger and held it to her fiercely to kill all of the other feelings this man produced in her. "Oh, no you don't," she said firmly. "I don't owe you anything."

"So, the lady's got an attitude. Just going with the tradition of the Pharrs?"

That struck her hard. "No, I'm just acting like a person who thanked you for what you did back there, and like a person who wants to get out of this hole. Why did you ever come into the cave at all? None of this would have happened if you'd stayed back. You should have gotten back on that yacht of yours—"

"Cruiser."

"What?"

"It's a cruiser, not a yacht."

"Whatever," she muttered, tensing as he came closer. "You should have just left on that…boat."

"I told you," he said softly, his eyes shadowed by the dim overhead light. "I don't deal with 'should haves' in this life. Not in any part of this life. That's a cop-out. I do what I have to do, and if it's wrong, I accept the consequences, like falling down a hole."

Maggie trembled and hugged herself harder, digging her fingers into her upper arms. "Consequences? Being trapped in some wine cellar?"

"Being trapped in a wine cellar with an ungrateful woman. I'd call that consequences."

The man used words better than anyone she'd ever

dealt with, and she hated him for that. She never could get her footing with him. "Why don't you tell me why you followed me? I told you I wanted to be alone."

For an instant, he almost looked taken aback, then she could see him gathering himself. "Okay, if you answer my question first."

"No, you tell me first."

He shrugged. "I wanted to apologize for what I said about freezing Sebastian Lake out if he found you. That's why I followed you into the cave."

Whatever she expected, it wasn't that, or his smile that caught on every nerve in her body. Damn him. She couldn't deal with it. It was safer to push past him and put some distance between them than to stand there in the glow of that smile. So she moved to one side, bumping into his shoulder in her effort to move away from him. She crossed to the door, touched the rough wood, then balled her hand up in a fist and hit the door as hard as she could.

"Hey, out there! We're trapped in here! Open the door! Hello? Is anyone there?" she screamed as loudly as she could.

As her voice died out, there was no sound through the thick wood. She exhaled and pressed her forehead to the wood as she closed her eyes. "I don't believe all this. I just wanted a quiet afternoon to explore the cove, then all hell breaks loose."

"Life never goes the way you think it will."

She scrunched her eyes more tightly shut as Connor spoke behind her. Her life sure hadn't gone the way she thought it would. If it had, she would have come down here, had her celebration with Amanda and gone back to accept Bill's marriage proposal and have a normal, average life. But Connor McKay had intruded and torn that picture apart.

She turned and Connor was there, right in front of her. His eyes were narrowed on her, then his hand lifted. Before she could think of what she was doing, she struck out and hit his hand away before it could touch her.

She saw the flash of pure anger on his face, then it was gone, as if it had never been. He didn't even rub the spot she'd hit, even though she could feel a tingling in her own hand from the impact.

"Sorry," he said, staring at her without blinking. She wished he'd scream instead of studying her like that. "It looks like it hurts."

"Of course it hurts," she said sharply. "And I've got a horrible headache." She suddenly realized that the last part was true. Her head was starting to pound. She touched her temple with the tips of her fingers. "And I'm starving."

"I doubt there's any food in here, but there's plenty to drink. Maybe you're just thirsty." He turned from her and crossed to the nearest wine rack. "Ah, only the best." He lifted a bottle of wine and studied the label. "A great year." He cast her a slanted glance. "Red or white?"

She pressed her fingers hard against her temple. "Neither. We couldn't even open a bottle if we wanted to."

"True. No corkscrew. We can't open the bottle, short of snapping the neck off, and that could get messy, glass bits and all," he said as he went farther down the rack. "Oh, perfect. Champagne. The cork comes out all by itself." He turned with a large bottle in his hand. "How about it? Thirsty?"

Those damned swim trunks all but disappeared in the soft light, and she had to blink to make sure he wasn't naked again. That was stupid, and it made her head hurt even more.

"It might help your headache. Or at least make you forget about it. How about it?"

She leaned back against the door and closed her eyes. "It's not cold."

"It doesn't have to be cold if it's good enough stuff. Cool is just fine."

"How much would that bottle cost?"

He looked down at it. "Not much—two, three hundred, maybe."

She couldn't begin to think of something you could drink costing that much money. "You can't just drink it. It's not ours."

"But you're forgetting that we both belong to the club, and anything we drink down here can just be put on our tab." He came toward her, the bottle in his hand. "I'll make you a deal. This one's on me. You can buy the next one. How about it?"

She stared at the man and the bottle, then shrugged. "Whatever."

Connor undid the bailing wire on the cork, then twisted it. Suddenly, it exploded. The cork shot out to strike the ceiling, while the sound echoed painfully in the enclosed room. Champagne gushed out of the neck of the bottle, but died down quickly before Connor lifted the bottle to his nose, inhaled for a moment, then looked at her. "It smells wonderful," he said, then tilted the bottle and took a long swallow. "It tastes wonderful, and worth every penny." He held the bottle out to her.

She hesitated, then reached for the bottle. It was

heavier than she would have thought, and elegantly formed with a wide bottom and a sweeping neck. With both hands, she tipped it up and took a small sip. The carbonation was as delicate as the taste, a slightly fruity dryness that tasted of grapes and freshness all at once.

She took a second drink before offering it back to Connor again. "You're right. That's wonderful," she said.

He took it back, took another long swallow, then turned with the bottle in his hand. "We're going to be here for a while," he said as he crossed to a space by the farthest rack. "We should get comfortable."

He disappeared behind the racks, then she heard him say, "I'll be dammed."

"What is it?" she asked from where she stood.

"A closet of some sort." She heard a creaking sound. "And dark as the pit."

"Look out for rats," she called to him.

She heard him chuckle, then he came back into sight carrying the bottle in his right hand, and with something hanging over his left arm. "No rats, just some stacks of material that smell old and vaguely of mothballs. I didn't even know anyone used them anymore."

Then he put the bottle on the floor by the far wall and shook out the material. It floated out in front of him onto the floor. "Come, sit and be comfortable," he said to her.

"I'm fine standing."

"Whatever," he said as he dropped down on the layers of fabric, which looked as if they'd once been navy or deep blue curtains. He reached for the bottle, gripping it as he scooted back against the wall, his long legs stretched out in front of him. Then he looked up at her as he held the bottle out. "More?"

She crossed and took the bottle, but kept standing as she took another drink. It went down her throat so nicely. She licked her lips, then leaned down to give it back to Connor. "That's very nice, even if it's not chilled."

"Delicate, smooth, with a definite hint of the grape," he said before he took another long drink. He leaned back against the wall with a deep sigh and rested the large bottle on his bare thigh. He looked up at her, his eyes narrowed. "Can I tell you that your bruise is getting darker without getting hit?"

"Don't be ridiculous," she said testily.

"Ridiculous? Do I add that to egotistical, stubborn, conceited and arrogant?"

"Would you stop that?" she said, and reached down to take the bottle out of his hand. "I need a drink," she muttered, and tipped it up to take a long swallow.

"Okay, I'll stop whatever it is you think I'm doing, if you answer my question."

"What question?" she asked.

"Why do you kiss me as if you want it, then you push me away, looking as if I scare the stuffing out of you. It's giving me a headache. It can't be because I'm me," he said, and that grin came out of nowhere. "I admit that I'm egotistical. That's a given. So, that can't be what's wrong."

She held so tightly to the bottle neck that she was surprised it didn't snap in her hand. "You're definitely egotistical," she agreed, and lifted the bottle to take another drink of it.

"Will you sit down?" he asked.

She put the bottle down and looked at him. "Why?"

"Why not? Just sit. Relax. And answer me."

Her legs were feeling a bit weird, probably the fall and then the long walk through the caves. Despite the fact that she wanted nothing better than to get farther from him, the only place to sit was on the old curtains.

"Okay," she said, sinking down on the musty fabric and drawing her legs around into a cross-legged position. She held the bottle out to Connor. "Here, it's your turn."

He leaned forward to take the bottle, then settled back with it, but he didn't take a drink. He just looked at her, and she wanted to block that look. So, she closed her eyes. There was silence, then he touched her. His finger tapped her knee, but it jolted her as much as if he'd hit her without warning.

She jerked back and met his gaze. But there was no smile there now, just a deep, dark frown that was reflected in his eyes. "God, what's wrong? I don't bite. It's not my style to play pirate and pillage and plunder."

She stared at him, the words on the tip of her tongue to tell him the truth, that she was a nobody. The kind of person he paid Fletcher good money to keep at arm's length. But the words wouldn't come. She couldn't say them. She couldn't stand the thought of him looking at her as if she were lower than the lowest. Not one of his kind. No, she couldn't do that.

No more than she could tell him she was so very close to falling in love with him. God, that would be so easy, so very easy with this man. No wonder every single woman in the world was after him. "I told you that I'm…I'm getting married," she whispered, clasping her hands tightly in her lap and praying for him to move back and away from her.

"Okay, we know that, but that doesn't explain why I scare you to death." He moved back and had the bottle in his hand again to hold it out to her. "Drink. Then we'll talk."

She drank more champagne, and all the while she could feel him watching her. That was horrible, that feeling of his eyes on her even when she wasn't looking at him. She took another drink, then put the bottle down on the floor between them.

He didn't move to take it, and the silence in the cellar was deafening. She couldn't stand that, either. "Why doesn't Fletch come and find you?" she said absently.

"He will. He's like the postal service. Neither snow, nor sleet, nor rain, nor the gloom of night shall stay him from his appointed rescuing."

"I don't think that's exactly how it goes."

"Close enough. And he will come. Sooner or later."

"A devoted bodyguard."

"I told you before, he's a lot of things. Bodyguard-cum-assistant. Chauffeur-cum-friend-cum-confidant. And last but not least, a man who sees all and tells nothing."

"He sounds better than a good dog," she said, shocking herself at how easily the joke came to her.

"Nice analogy," he replied with a fleeting smile.

"How about your family? Is there anyone down here to come looking for you, too?"

He raked his fingers through his hair, spiking it

slightly around his face. "No family, not here or any-where."

"None?"

"Oh, cousins, distant, very distant. An aunt. A godfather. That's about it."

"I'm sorry," she said without thinking.

"There's nothing to be sorry about. I've been on my own for a lot of years. I didn't get to where I am on family money, not like most of the Pharrs. It's not old money, it's earned money." He reached for the bottle and took a swallow before resting it on his thigh again. "What about your family?"

At least she could tell him the truth about that. "Mother, father, two brothers, one sister. All younger than me, all still at home, except me."

"No half sisters and half brothers, or stepbrothers and sisters?"

"No."

"Your parents are still married?"

"For thirty-one years."

"I'll drink to that," he said, taking another drink before leaning forward to offer the bottle to her. "In our circles, that's just plain amazing," he said as she took the bottle from him.

"It's called commitment."

"But you have to admit that around here, it's pretty rare."

"In my circle, it's not that unusual." She took a drink, then said, "Maybe you've been hanging out in the wrong circles."

He chuckled at that. "Oh, I think my circles are pretty good."

Thankfully, the champagne was easing more than her headache. She could feel the tension leaving her, even when he talked about his circles. "Is that really important to you?"

"It's important to know who you're around. It's just easier and safer to be with people who don't give a damn about money or position, because they have both." He shrugged. "I told you that I've had my share of the others. Thank goodness Fletch takes care of that for me."

"He's good at what he does."

He smiled slightly. "Sorry about that. He thought you were a crazy who'd found out where I was, then decided to make a beachfront assault." The smile shifted. "What were you doing there?"

She actually laughed at that, and it felt good to ease the tension a bit more. "Well, I sure wasn't planning a beachfront assault, or an air strike or a nuclear blast. I was just swimming and got confused about where I was going." She took a breath, then, without thinking about her words, blurted out, "I heard that you had a woman sky dive into your house."

He rested his head back against the wall and sighed. "Yes, I did. You read about that in the press?"

She couldn't actually remember where she'd read it, or if she'd seen it on the news. "I don't remember."

"Did you hear that she was naked and saying she wanted to have my children?"

She almost choked on the drink she'd been taking. "You're kidding!"

"I don't have my hand up, do I?" he asked, his lids lowered to shadow his eyes. "There haven't been any nuclear assaults yet." He looked around them. "And no one's ever used the old trapped-in-the-wine-cellar-after-falling-in-a-hole attack before. Very original."

He was smiling, but it suddenly wasn't funny for Maggie. "I wasn't trying to do anything like that."

He raised his hand. "Sorry. I forgot. I was joking." He slowly lowered his hand, eyeing her steadily. "Did you ever think that maybe I'm the one who planned it?"

"Of course you didn't," Maggie said. "That's ridiculous. You don't need tricks to get a woman. I mean, to just..." She held the bottle of champagne out to him. She hadn't drunk that much, but it was making it hard for her to find words that didn't sound horrible. "You know what I mean."

He took a drink before saying, "Even I can use help once in a while, especially when the going gets chilly." He held out his free hand palm out to her. "Sorry. I didn't mean that." He held the bottle up. "It's the champagne talking. Bottom line," he said as he rested the bottle on his thigh. "You can't run away from me if we're locked in on both sides by doors that won't cooperate."

"I don't run away from you," she said, but without a lot of conviction.

"Don't you? How about on the beach last night? How about this morning? You got out of my house so fast, I barely saw the blur as you went through the gates. And how about your disappearing act at lunch? If that isn't a pattern for you, I don't know what is."

"A pattern you aren't used to, either, from what I've heard."

He laughed at that, a rough sound that echoed

slightly in the small space. "You know, you really should know better than to believe everything you read in the press."

"They get things right some of the time," she said.

"Very seldom." He exhaled harshly and drank more, then put the bottle down and got to his feet. "Empty. How about another one, this one on you?" he asked.

Even with foggy thinking, the idea of paying hundreds of dollars for a bottle of champagne made her wince. "I don't think I—"

He cut off her words as he crossed to the rack and took out another bottle. He uncorked it and came back to where they sat, holding it out to her as if she hadn't started to say anything. She stared at the bottle as he said, "A different label, but it should be acceptable."

She took the bottle. "How much?"

"About the same," he said. "Maybe a bit more. It's a more limited label. Hopefully as good."

It was open, and even she knew that you didn't recork champagne. She'd worry about payment later. She took a sip. "It's good, but I always thought you had to chill champagne."

"Chilling makes 'good' 'great.' When we get out of here, let me show you the joys of really chilled champagne."

The offer was made casually, almost indifferently by him, but for Maggie it brought back the fact that when they got out of here, she wouldn't be anywhere around Connor again. She looked at him and knew that maybe it was pride, or maybe it was wanting to salvage some of the fantasy, but she never wanted him to know who she really was.

She never wanted him to look at her with disgust or distrust. No, she wanted the look in his eyes to stay as long as it could, and when it was gone, she'd be gone. That thought made her stomach knot slightly.

"How about it?" Connor asked.

She put down the bottle and ignored his question. "So, tell me the lies they tell about you."

"The lies don't matter, what matters is the women who believe them. That I'm some sort of Prince Charming who can be 'caught' and make their lives a fantasy." He reached for the bottle. "That's when they go crazy."

Maybe they got crazy because he was so sexy, it was like being around a fire when he was close. They weren't crazy at all. "Yeah, crazy," she said softly.

He was looking at her, she could feel it, but she didn't look at him. She stared at the bottle he held, the smear of her fingerprints mingled with his on it in the clinging dust. "Only someone who's been there can understand it," he said. "Only someone who's seen the craziness can appreciate how hard it is to deal with."

"Another reason to stay with your own kind?" she asked.

"That sounds like another indictment," he murmured.

She looked at him, at a man who looked more endearing with the passing of time. "I'm sorry," she said, touching her tongue to her lips and tasting the champagne there. She shifted on the fabric, felt a bit lightheaded, and twisted until she was back against the wall, inches from where Connor leaned against the stones. It made it much easier for her not to be facing him right then. With a sigh, she rested against the cold wall and said, "I seem to have a penchant for sarcasm." But only with him.

"I never would have guessed," he said dryly, and she could sense him moving, taking another drink. "Are you sarcastic with William Rome?"

The alcohol was doing its job. Even the mention of Bill's name didn't cause her to flinch at the lies she'd been telling. "No, I'm not."

"Love does strange things to people, doesn't it?" he said softly.

She settled into a muzzy place, where things seemed so much better. Things like love, and that love involving Connor McKay. She had to be a bit drunk, but it didn't stop the oddly wonderful feeling of being right next to a man she loved. The thought was there, as simple as that, and she hugged it around her. A fantasy. Yes, love did strange things to people. It even made them believe in the impossible.

Chapter Eleven

Connor drank more champagne and wished it was whiskey. Champagne was working way too slowly for him. Now that Margaret had moved next to him, leaning against the wall and pushing her long, slender legs out on the fabric, he couldn't ignore the fact that he should have torn down the door to get out if that's what it took. Staying here with her like this was just making things worse.

He couldn't even remember why he'd given up so easily on getting out. Had he thought that if she was close to him, he could talk her out of whatever she had going with William Rome? Fool. He knew now that the only thing he'd wanted was to be close to her, and that closeness wasn't for talking.

He took another drink. "Old Sebastian must be turning in his grave," he mumbled. "To think they made his dungeons into wine cellars."

She moved beside him, then she was taking the bottle from his hand. He glanced at her, at the soft beauty she possessed even with no makeup and her hair wild with curls. "Old Sebastian wouldn't be surprised by anything," she said just before she tipped the bottle up and took a long drink. "He'd probably just join right in and get rip-roaring drunk."

"What'd they drink back then?" he asked.

"Mead? Ale? Wine, for sure." She actually giggled, a soft, airy sound. "Certainly not three hundred dollar champagne. Or maybe this champagne would have been too new to drink back then."

He loved the sound of her laughter and would have done anything to hear it again. But what he had on his mind when he looked at her wasn't funny. Not funny at all. And his body was letting him know just how it was affecting him to notice the way her high breasts rose and fell under the skimpy halter top. When she started to lift the bottle to her lips, he found himself stopping her. She was getting drunk, nicely, but still drunk, and he suddenly didn't want her to be anything but sober. He wanted this softness without the aid of alcohol. "Maybe you've had enough," he said.

"I'm fine," she said in a breathy voice, and took another drink. "Tepid champagne. Lovely."

"I told you, chilled this would be a killer."

"How about if you froze it?"

"Frozen champagne? I don't know. I didn't think you can freeze alcohol, can you?"

"I don't know." She giggled softly. "Champagne ice cubes. What a novel idea. If I could freeze a pirate, I could certainly chill this stuff." She giggled, and he saw her press her hand to her mouth.

He took in everything about her, the way her eyes danced with humor, the sweep of her throat, the way the curls rested on her naked shoulders. Lovely. Breathtaking. "Don't do that," he said, not daring a touch on her hand. "I like it when you laugh."

Even in the low light, he could see the color flood her face as she slowly lowered her hand. "Giggling in Sebastian Lake's dungeons," she whispered in a vaguely slurred voice.

"A great use for this place."

She studied him from under those ridiculously long lashes. "You know," she began, "if you had an eye patch, a few scars from battle, you'd look a lot like Sebastian Lake."

"I can get an eye patch, and I can assure you, I've got quite a few battle scars." He touched her shoulder, just making contact with the tip of his finger. It pleased him that she didn't draw back or try to hit him. She trembled at the contact. Yes, that pleased him a lot. "But I can assure you that I seldom pillage and plunder, and never…never take a woman against her will."

"You wouldn't have to," she said on a low whisper. "The Ultimate Catch…" She touched her tongue to her lips again, a habit of hers when she was uncertain, he'd finally figured out. And the sight of it was running riot through him. "Any woman would…" Her voice trailed off, and when she lifted the bottle again, Connor touched it to keep her from taking a drink.

"No, you've had enough."

She didn't draw back from him, and the look in her eyes when he met her gaze was like a jolt of electricity. "You could have any woman in the world," she said softly.

"I don't want just any woman," he said, not finishing it with the thought in his mind. The only woman he wanted was her. And he couldn't remember ever wanting any other woman as much as he wanted her right then.

"Oh, of course you don't," Maggie said, the champagne making her thoughts soft and very seductive. "You want someone who is like you."

"No, I don't. The last thing I want is a woman who's six feet tall, gets a five o'clock shadow and sings in baritone." Connor grinned at her. "No, that's a far cry from what I want in a woman."

The laughter he thought would come didn't. And that stopped him dead.

"I know what you don't want," she said in a voice so low he could barely hear her.

His grin faded as quickly as the laughter in her had died. "What are you talking about?" he asked.

"That…that girl who sky dived to meet you. Did…did you ever…you know, just meet her? Or did you talk to the…the one in your bed?"

"No, Fletch took care of them and got them out of there."

She looked at him, the alcohol making the impact of those dark eyes seem as if they were the night. As if she could just get lost in them and be anything she wanted to be. What Connor wanted. She licked her lips. "You know…you should have just met one of them. She might…you could have found out she…she was really nice and just thought you were really nice, and that she never thought about the money or the…" She waved her hand vaguely. "You know, all that stuff. The pool…cut in half…the fountain…things…"

"You're a bit drunk, aren't you?" he whispered as he leaned toward her.

She giggled, and wished that she hadn't. But the

giggle was just there, as surely as her feelings for
Connor. She could feel his body heat at her side, and
the desire to just melt into him was overwhelming.
Too seductive. "I didn't...I wasn't hungry, and
lunch..." She giggled again, and put her hand over
her mouth.

Connor was there, almost in front of her, and his
hand was on hers, gently tugging it down from her
lips. "I told you, I like that," he said softly. Then
his hand let go of hers and his fingers touched her
cheek. "A lot."

His image was so clear to her at that moment,
despite the low light and the champagne. She saw
every detail of the man. Fine lines fanning at the
corners of his eyes, the flare of his nostrils with each
breath, the seductive curve of his lips. And his eyes.
She reached out to him, finding the heat of his cheek
under her palm. "You have...the most wonderful
eyes," she whispered, shocking herself as the words
came out, but not stopping them. "Dark as
night...and so...so..." She couldn't find the words.
"You...you just..."

She couldn't even focus on her thoughts when his
fingers trailed along her cheek to her throat, then
slowly slipped onto the nape of her neck. She was
lost and she knew it. But she didn't care. Nothing
mattered but his touch and his closeness, and the way
he was looking at her lips. Nothing.

"What...what do you...think of libar...?" She
swallowed to try to make her lips work. "Librarians?" she said with great slowness and care to get
the word out.

"Librarians?" he asked. "I've never thought
about librarians at all," he admitted. "No interest

there.'' His smile, shadowed his mouth, teasing and tormenting her at the same time. ''But I've thought a lot about you.''

She trembled when he shifted closer, his breath fanning her face. ''But, I...I'm a...'' She couldn't remember what she was when he was this close, when she felt as if all she had to do was move to him and she'd be lost in him. The librarian would be lost. The woman who had never traveled, who had been in awe of a home he took so casually, the woman who had a life she wasn't sure she wanted to go back to. She'd be gone, and the woman who could love this man would be all that was left. A woman who ached with a need for him that had become a raging hunger.

His fingers shifted, tangling in her hair, and his eyes narrowed. ''Your poor head,'' he whispered. ''And your hand.'' His other hand brushed her hand resting on her thigh. ''You're the walking wounded.''

She chuckled softly at that and turned her hand over, tangling her fingers with his. ''I couldn't walk right now.''

''Then it's a good thing you're right here, sitting down,'' he said. ''No headache?''

''No.''

''Champagne, the miracle medicine.''

No, Connor McKay, the miracle man, she thought, and hesitantly touched his bare chest. His heart beat beneath her fingertips, and that sense of losing herself in him was growing as the world blurred and lost all the sharp edges. ''A miracle,'' she breathed. Being here with him was a miracle. Him looking at her like this, touching her, was a miracle.

"Thank you," he said, his voice vibrating against her hand.

"What for?" she asked unsteadily.

"For not hitting me when I touched you." The smile was achingly endearing, and faltered slightly as he said, "I can take abuse, but when it comes to someone like you…" His eyes dropped to her lips. "God, William Rome is a lucky man."

"He's a banker," she said.

He leaned toward her, brushed his lips fleetingly over hers, a simple action, yet so devastating to her. Whatever barriers she might have been able to muster crumbled completely. She knew she shouldn't let Connor touch her and that she shouldn't have touched him, but there was nothing in her to fight with. His hand on her was so welcome, so needed by her, that she didn't fight it. The champagne had softened things, made them less hard and harsh to her, and that softening let her forget about lies and the fact that she shouldn't be there with him.

She went into his arms willingly, resting her head on his chest, just listening to his heartbeat for a long moment. She thought of stopping all of this, but when Connor tipped her head back and touched her lips again with his, that thought was gone.

She tasted him, opening her mouth, welcoming his invasion, suddenly filled with a hunger for him that was raw and painfully elemental. He caught her at her waist, lifting her to ease her around into his lap, then she was facing him, her arms going around his neck and her legs around his waist.

The world ground to a stop, and every atom of her being centered on the man in front of her. The man touching her.

"I can't do this," he whispered roughly. "You're more than a little drunk."

She didn't want to hear that, not now, when all she wanted was to be closer than possible to this man. She moved closer to him, then lifted her lips to his, and nothing else mattered. Her arms circled his neck, and the next thing she knew, she was in his arms, his mouth exploring hers, his tongue tracing her teeth, tasting her, leaving his taste in her.

It was so easy to just exist with him, to forget about sanity and reality, to feel his skin against her, to feel his heat mingling with hers. Lies and logic meant nothing as she tried to get closer than was humanly possible with Connor. She wanted to melt into him, to lose herself in him and never have to be without him again. His taste and touch filled her, and as his hands skimmed down her back, cupping her bottom to pull her harder against him, she gasped. He wanted her as much as she wanted him. She could feel his need pressing against her, and a resistance in him that puzzled her.

The champagne had freed her, letting her release all of her pain and worry, allowing her to let go of all of her sane reasons for not doing this. It gave her the sense that anything could happen. When he buried his lips in her neck, when he whispered "Damn it, this is crazy," when his lips burned her throat, she gave in to the explosions of pleasure.

Then her arms circled his neck, and when she felt him easing her back and down, she shifted with him until she was on the hard floor and he was over her.

Connor was braced over her by one hand, and she strained toward him, toward need and desire, toward sensations that mingled with fantasies and desires

that swirled around and through her. Desire was
ready to explode in her. But when she was certain
his hand was going to slip between material and skin,
when the saltiness of his skin touched her tongue,
everything turned wrong.

He was trying to move back, whispering something about things being wrong, very wrong, and he
wouldn't do it. She didn't understand and tried to
keep a hold on him, but he was breaking contact
gently but insistently, grasping her arms and easing
them back from him. Then he was leaning over her,
receding into the blur above her, and she could feel
the shaking in his body.

"Connor, what…" She tried to focus, but with
him leaning over her, that was almost impossible.

He was at one side of her, sitting by her, one hand
pressed to the floor by her shoulder, the other touching her cheek. He was shaking. "No, I can't. Not
like this."

A chill cut through the haze. "You don't
want…want to…" She couldn't even use the word
love. Her eyes burned and the alcohol was bitter in
her throat.

"Oh, damn it, that's just it. I do. I want you, but
this is all wrong." She shuddered as he jerked his
hand away. "I told you, I never take a woman
against her will, especially not a woman who has
someone waiting for her."

She was shaking, too, but from the cold that suddenly surrounded her and the mention of her lies.
"You aren't…I don't…."

"You're drunk." He pulled even farther back
from her. "You don't have any will right now." He
took a ragged breath. "I barely do."

She had never felt more empty, or more unable to think and focus in her life. The lovely champagne of moments ago was the enemy now. She tried to move back but could barely make her hands brace herself.

Foolish. Stupid, she thought, realizing how crazy she'd been moments ago. She didn't belong here, and thank God, Connor knew that. That he was smart enough to stop this before it was too late. She should be thankful, she thought as she fumbled for the wall, needing it to help keep her sitting.

It was the champagne and being half drunk. Very drunk. That was why she wasn't crying, why she wasn't shattering from humiliation. Just shaking, and feeling disoriented.

With trembling hands, she pulled her legs up and to her chest and held on to them. Pressing her forehead to her knees, she closed her eyes tightly.

When he touched her shoulder, she gasped, "No, don't." She jerked forward, scrambling to her feet on legs that felt decidedly weak, and kept her back to him. She looked around, but there was no escape, so she stood where she was, not daring to turn around. She couldn't look at him. She couldn't pull that off at all, not after the way she'd thrown herself at him.

"I'm sorry," he whispered behind her.

"Please, no, just…just…" She bit her lip so hard she thought she tasted the metallic tinge of blood on her lips mingling with his essence still there. She shivered violently and hugged her arms around herself. "It's the…the champagne," she whispered.

Then she saw the bottle by her feet, just sitting there, taunting her, and she reached down to pick it up. It was all the bottle's fault. She had to amend that. Not completely. She'd wanted that kiss, that touching. She'd wanted it on a soul-deep level, but the champagne had just made it easier to forget. But that was impossible.

Connor was there, standing right behind her, and he was reaching for the bottle over her shoulder, being careful not to touch her. "Let me have that," he said, his hot breath touching her bare skin.

He was touching the top of the bottle, but she had it tightly in her hand at the flare below the neck. She moved abruptly, getting away from Connor and the heat that he brought with him. Then she lifted the bottle and was going to throw it into the shadows, but Connor was too fast for her. He grabbed it, his body pressed to her back in the process, and her grip on the bottle was released.

"You don't want any more," he whispered near her left ear, obviously thinking she was going to drink even more.

She turned, almost hitting her shoulder on the bottle, which Connor held now, but he jerked back. She stared at him. God, she could tell how close he'd been to the edge, right there with her, and he'd stopped it all. Even worse, he wasn't doing a thing to hide the evidence of his response.

"You...you don't know what I want," she said tightly, trying as hard to ignore the sight of him in the indecently skimpy swim trunks as she had when she thought he'd been naked.

"You want your William Rome," he stated flatly. "All you need to do is to tell the guy you lost your head, got drunk and crazy with another man."

Oh, she was drunk, all right, but Bill would never know. No more than he'd ever know anything about

Connor. No one would. Her eyes burned, and she realized that she was close to tears as the champagne let the pain start to grow in her. Not even the alcohol could stop it.

"That…thatsh…" She swallowed hard, stunned that despite the fact that she hadn't taken another drink, she was feeling more and more drunk all the time. Delayed reaction? Her lips barely worked. "Thash dishgusting," she managed to say.

"You're drunk. This doesn't count. Rome never needs to know, and you don't need to justify it with me."

Oh, it counted for her. But she knew it wouldn't with Connor. He'd forget. She'd be gone and he'd forget. She just wished she could. But she never would. "I…I don't have to jushtif…" She licked her lips. "Justineye…" That was wrong, as wrong as it had been to let him touch her the very first time. "Just-if-eye," she said with painful slowness. "Not anything to anyone."

"Damn straight," he muttered, then took a drink from the bottle he'd taken from her.

"Hey, I…I paid for that…tons and tons of money for it."

She reached for the bottle, caught it by the neck and grabbed it from him, with no idea what she was going to do with it when she had it. Then everything changed. Something was happening, and it took her a full heartbeat to realize there were voices close by.

"Oh, my, you were right."

She slowly lowered the bottle as she turned toward the door that was miraculously opening. She thought the alcohol was making her hallucinate, making her see Hill, the waiter from the restaurant, standing in the open door staring at her. Then, right behind him, came the big man, Connor's shadow, Fletch.

Fletch looked in, and as if he was used to finding his boss in a wine cellar with a very drunk woman, he nodded slightly. "Should I have the car brought around?"

Maggie stared at the man, then suddenly she was giggling, laughing so hard that she knew she was crying. If Connor hadn't grabbed the champagne bottle again, she would have dropped it on the floor. "Bring...bring the car around?" she gasped through fits of laughter. "Bring the car around?"

"Margaret?" Connor was saying from a great distance, but when she looked at him, the tears of laughter blurred him. "Margaret, it's okay," he said.

"It's relief," Fletch was saying somewhere off to the side. "It's like shock, a spontaneous reaction to being rescued."

"No, it's called drunk," Connor said with a tinge of annoying humor in his tone.

Maggie moved back until she finally felt the solid support of the wall behind her and slowly slid down to sit on the floor. Thankfully, the fits of laughter were starting to dissolve. "Damn champagne," she muttered thickly. "Rotten...mishera..."

He was right in front of her, hunkering down, then his fingertip softly skimmed over the dampness on her cheek. "This is all my fault," he said, and there was no laughter in those eyes now. "Just forget it. We're free. That's what counts."

There was a horrible ache in her middle, and she swiped her hand at his, but he moved before she could make contact. "You're...you're worse than old Sebashtian...Sebas...that pirate, ever was."

"No, I never take a woman against her will, re-member?" he said in a low, rough voice, then talked loudly without looking over his shoulder. "Get us some robes, anything to cover up, and make damned sure no one knows we're here."

Maggie clenched her hands into fists on her knees and glared at Connor as Fletch spoke to Hill. "You heard the man, and keep quiet, okay?"

"Yes, sir," the man said, then he left.

"You arrogant bash...bastard," she hissed.

Connor didn't move. Instead, he talked to Fletch again. "You've got the car?"

"Yes, boss."

"Good. We're taking this lady home."

"Oh, no you're not," she gasped, and awkwardly tried to stand, pushing against the floor with one hand and grabbing blindly for the wall with the other. Con-nor stood and moved back just a bit, giving her room, and when she finally got on her feet, she realized the room was moving. Just sort of spinning slowly, but only going forward, just the way she was falling for-ward without trying.

The next thing she knew, she was back in Con-nor's arms, swaying into his chest, supported against his body. This was okay to be here. She was drunk, and if Connor wasn't holding her up, she'd be flat on her face on the stone. Another bubble of laughter started to rise inside her, until she looked up and his face was just inches from hers.

He looked down at her, and in a whisper, he said, "Just let me get you home, then my conscience is clear."

"I...I can walk," she managed to say, but with little to no conviction in her voice.

"No walking wounded. If you tried, you'd fall flat on your beautiful face. Trust me, I've seen drunk, and you're way past simple drunk. Way past it."

She could feel her head getting more and more muzzy, her thoughts blurred and running together. What did it matter? He could take her back to Amanda's house. That was okay. It didn't matter at all.

"Here you go, sir," someone was saying, then terry cloth surrounded her. A robe, she thought, all white and fluffy and soft. Then someone else was holding her shoulders. But before she could turn to see who had her, Connor had her again. She sagged into him, against more soft terry cloth, and the steady beating of his heart against her cheek.

"Pay…the bill," she mumbled.

Laughter rumbled against her and surrounded her.

"Remember, no bills."

Then she felt herself being swooped up and into Connor's arms. She didn't fight it at all.

"Time to break out of this place."

"You know, you…you're so…damned… damned…"

"I'm not drunk," he said.

"No, shtubborn," she mumbled thickly.

"Damn straight," he said.

"Okay, you win…for now," she said.

Connor felt Margaret snuggle into his arms, a complete surrender on her part and a wonderfully satisfactory one. It almost countered the frustration he'd felt just moments ago when he'd realized how wrong making love to her then would have been. No, he couldn't think of that right now. He wasn't a noble man, but with Margaret, nobility seemed a given for him. He wouldn't think of the stark fact that she would have let him have her only because she'd been drunk and William Rome was nowhere around.

Chapter Twelve

Connor rested his chin on her soft curls then looked at Fletch and the waiter by the door.

"Don't even ask," he muttered. "Just get us out of here without anyone seeing us."

"I brought the Mercedes," Fletch said. "Maybe I should try to get a hotel car, or—"

"The Mercedes is fine," he said, then looked at the waiter. "My man will take good care of you to make very sure no one hears about this, is that understood?"

"Oh my, yes, sir, of course. This never happened. That's no problem at all."

"Good," Connor said, and strode with Maggie in his arms toward the door. When he got up to Fletch, he looked at the big man. "Okay, just where in the hell are we?"

"In a separate building to the south of the Fortress, a supplemental wine cellar, storage area." He nodded to the waiter. "The man's a treasure trove of trivia about Lake. When I found the cruiser..." He shrugged. "I'll explain that later, but this guy came up with the idea you'd gone right through the maze down there. Or that you were trapped by the collapse.

So, he brought me here to go in the back entrance to the tunnels.''

"Thanks," Connor said to both men, then motioned to Fletch to get going. The big man led the way into a short corridor lined with wooden doors and softly lit sconces, up several worn stone steps and out into dusky light. "What time is it?" Connor asked as he stepped onto a stone path that cut through luxuriant gardens and was topped by slender palms.

"Just past eight. Four hours past Gunner's call," Fletch said as he started down the path and the waiter fell into step behind Connor.

Gunner? The man hadn't entered his thoughts since he'd spotted Margaret at the cave. Connor looked off to the right, at the Fortress ablaze with lights against the dim sky. Even from this distance, he could see people swarming all over the place, probably getting ready for the big celebration the next night.

They walked parallel with the beach far below, under palms, while the waiter fussed behind Connor. "Sir, are you all right?" he asked every few steps. "Can you manage? Do you need help?"

"I'm just fine," he said more than once, and when Fletch glanced back at him, Connor flicked his head toward the waiter. Fletch understood immediately and moved back to where the waiter was, stopping him with a hand on his shoulder. "I think we can take it from here," Fletch said, and took a number of bills out of his pocket to press them into the man's hand. "Just tell me where you can have the car brought to that won't draw attention from anyone."

"Yes, sir," he said as Connor stood there with a sleeping Maggie in his arms. The waiter pointed down the way they'd been going. "Follow this path and you'll come to a storage area. Beyond that is a lower parking lot where the employees usually park."

"How soon can you get our car there?"

"Five minutes, sir."

"Get going," Fletch said, and the waiter headed up a higher path and out of sight.

Fletch looked at Connor. "Want me to carry her, boss?" he asked.

Connor shifted Margaret in his arms, but he wasn't about to give her up. Not just yet. "Let's just get to the car," he said, knowing that this might be the last time he'd be able to hold Margaret in his arms. And he wasn't going to give it up easily.

CONNOR FOLLOWED FLETCH along the lower path, then went around a series of metal storage buildings and out onto an asphalt parking lot hidden from the rest of the area by high box hedges. The Mercedes convertible came into sight as they stepped onto the pavement, then the waiter pulled it up right beside Connor. He got out and came around, fussing as Connor slipped into the passenger seat, maneuvering Margaret until she was on his lap, her bare feet on the center console.

Fletch got behind the wheel, and the waiter closed the door with a solid thud. He touched the door frame. "Sir, we are so glad that you are both okay. When Mr. Jones came to tell me what happened, it was very stressful. But thank goodness you knew enough to keep going and get to the room. Anyone else would have been trapped down there."

"I didn't know anything. She did."

"Ah, the lady is very well versed with regard to old Sebastian and his haunts," he said with a smile.

"Yes, very," Connor said, then motioned to Fletch.

Fletch gunned the motor and the waiter spoke quickly. "Take the left turn, that's the lower drive, and you won't have to go past the guest area."

Fletch waved a hand at him, then gunned the motor again and drove off, cutting away from the main drive onto a narrow lane that came out near the open front gates. As they moved onto the road, Margaret shifted and she pressed her hand to Connor's heart. He felt her sigh, shuddering slightly before she settled again.

He closed his eyes tightly as every atom of his being responded to her. Now wasn't the time for this.

"Do I get an explanation?" Fletch finally asked as he drove them toward the Pharr house.

"No, other than to say I'm glad I pay you big bucks to be so smart."

The big man laughed. "Yeah, sure, big bucks. And it was simple deduction. I got a skiff from the caretaker, looked down the coast the way you went and spotted the cruiser in the cove. Since you weren't there, I figured you'd gone into the cave. I found the collapsed path and an empty hole, so I figured you'd gotten out and kept going."

"Then why didn't you come in the back way?"

"I wasn't taking any chances getting myself trapped. How in the hell did you manage to find that wine cellar?"

"Margaret figured it out."

He cast Connor a glance, then turned back to the road. "Are you going to make me ask why she was chugging a bottle of champagne when that door opened?''

Connor rested his head against the high back seat and looked at the night sky overhead. "She was getting very drunk, and cutting me dead."

"Oh, sure, boss. That'll be the day."

"I'm serious."

"No way. When's the last time you had a woman say no to you?"

"About fifteen minutes ago," he muttered.

"Damn, she's a feisty one, isn't she?"

Connor chuckled at that. "Very."

Margaret moved on his lap again, shifting around until she settled once more with a sigh. Her hand moved from his chest, catching at the lapel of the robe, then, without him realizing what she was doing, she slipped her hand under the terry cloth and rested her palm on his chest, then her cheek on the fabric over her hand. A simple action of trust, but it made him tense, and when he tensed, it was obvious just what sort of tensing his body was going through.

He was the one to shift this time, moving to one side just a bit and staring hard at the night around them. "Gunner," he said quickly. "Tell me about Gunner." Business would divert him from the woman in his embrace, if anything would.

"The man didn't buy the fact that you were late. He thinks you're playing a game, but he was too controlled to accuse me of lying. He did let it slip that he'd talked to *a friend,* who told him you were having a good time down here. Now, he's getting worried. Do you suppose Lars, his good friend, is actually helping you out without knowing it?"

He was relaxing a bit, and he exhaled with relief. "I could use all the help I can get."

"Naw, you're good. Damned good."

"He's stubborn," Margaret said suddenly, the words muffled but totally understandable.

Connor looked down at her, but her eyes were closed and her hair was stirring in the breeze. The bruise at her temple was ugly, but not as bad as he'd thought, and dirt was smeared around it.

"Smart woman," Fletch said.

Her hand on his chest shifted as she rubbed her forehead on the terry cloth. "No...dumb..." she mumbled. "So...so...dumb."

"No, you're not," Connor said, tempted to rock her in his arms, but instead just pressed a kiss carefully to the darkened swelling. "You got us out of there."

"But... but...we almost..." She shuddered and twisted her head away from his chest, but she still leaned back against his shoulder. "Where are we?"

Fletch pulled up to the closed gates at the Pharr estate and reached out to touch the call button on the intercom. "Yes?" a woman's voice said over the intercom.

"Pauline, it's Fletch. We've got your houseguest with us."

"Oh, come right up," the voice over the speaker said.

"You're home," Connor said. "You're safe."

Maggie knew she was safe, but it had nothing to do with coming to this place. It was Connor, being this close to Connor, being in his arms. But even through the alcoholic haze, she knew that was ridiculous. How safe had she been just a short time ago in his arms? No, that was a danger that was frightening.

As the car stopped, she tried to push away from Connor and sit up, but her head was swimming and her eyes wouldn't focus on anything, just a blur of dimness. And for a moment she thought they were back in the caves. Then she inhaled and took in the essence of Connor and the freshness of the night, and she knew they were free. No, they were out of that room, in the car, at Amanda's. But he was still so close to her, treacherously close.

If she could have gotten some balance, she would have insisted on getting out on her own, but just the simple act of trying to sit up left her head spinning. She sank back weakly in his arms, then closed her eyes as he managed to get out of the car while holding her. He was walking, and Fletch was saying something about a Gunner person. Gunner. She'd heard the name but couldn't begin to remember who he was.

Then she recognized the voice of the maid. "Oh, my Lord, what happened to the poor girl?"

"The poor girl has had too much champagne to drink," Connor said, his voice rumbling against her.

"Oh, my," the woman breathed. "But she's dirty, and her head… Oh, my."

"She's okay, believe me. The bump on her head's fine. She'll clean up very well, and she just needs to sleep it off."

"Oh, my goodness," Pauline gasped. "It's you."

"Yes, it's me," Connor said. "Now, where can I put her so she'll be comfortable?"

"Her suite is up the stairs and to the right," the maid said, then Connor was moving with her.

They were going up steps, and there was less light here, less of the glow coming through her eyelids. "In here, sir," Pauline said.

After a few steps, Connor stopped, then slowly lowered her onto cool linen. She rolled away from him, the contact severed, but then it came back for a moment in the form of his hand, warmth brushing her cheek. "Make sure she has a few aspirin and plenty of tomato juice when she wakes up, and something to put on that bruise."

"Oh, yes, sir," Pauline said.

Maggie could sense Connor there for a long moment, but she didn't dare look up at him. If she did, there was no telling how foolishly she'd act. So she kept her eyes closed and held her breath, not daring to move when he whispered in her ear, "You can't keep running."

She shuddered as his lips touched her cheek.

"Take care of her," he said from farther away, then the door closed.

She sank into the linen, just letting go. *You can't keep running* echoed in her mind as she started to slip away into the soft, inviting darkness of sleep. Echoing just the way the voices had in the cave. Over and over until she was in a place where she didn't have to remember. She was safe from Connor there, at least for a while.

CONNOR STAYED UP MOST of the night working, trying to lose himself in the problems that at any other time would have been stimulating and challenging. But now they seemed an annoyance, and anything after being with Margaret came up second best.

When he finally slept, then woke just after dawn,

he dressed in chino slacks and a white shirt that he left open before he went barefoot down to the office.

Fletch was already there, putting papers into the fax machine, and he glanced at Connor when he came into the room. "Good morning."

Connor crossed to the desk and looked down at the memos. "What's going on?"

"Nothing. No calls, no faxes yet. Gunner's gearing up for the assault. He is not a happy man." Fletch turned from the fax machine and eyed Connor. "He'll never believe you didn't do that on purpose."

"I don't care what he believes," Connor muttered as he crossed to the windows and looked out at the early morning. "Send that waiter from the Fortress something to sweeten the pot."

"Sure, boss. So, what's the game plan?"

To put an end to the Margaret obsession, he thought. He turned to Fletch. "Find out about a William Rome. He's in banking, probably associated with the Pharrs."

"He's involved with Gunner?"

"No, nothing to do with Gunner. He's a friend of Margaret's. I want to know about him. Find out if he's into something with the Pharrs where it would be beneficial to both parties to merge."

"Merge?"

He grimaced. "As in marry."

"Anything else?"

"Find out how Margaret is today, if she survived the ordeal intact." He didn't feel as if he had, and he hadn't even awakened with a hangover. "Ask that friend of yours over there, the maid, Pauline."

"Why don't you do that?" Fletch asked.

He wanted to, if only he could look at Margaret

without wanting her, he thought. The phone rang and Fletch reached for it. "McKay Tech." After a long moment, he looked at Connor and mouthed, "Gunner."

He reached for the phone. "Gunner?"

The voice was controlled, but he could hear the annoyance that was underlying the tone. "You never got back to me."

"I know. I got tied up."

"Sure, and without your cell phone?"

At any other time, he would have played the game and probably brought the man to his knees, but right then he didn't have the patience or the taste for game playing. Instead he said, "I was trapped in a wine cellar with a beautiful woman until late last night."

There was silence on the other end, then a jarring bark of laughter. "Okay, don't tell me. Just give me an answer on our mutual problem."

Connor closed his eyes and knew what he should be doing instead of talking to Gunner. "I don't have the time right now. I need to go and check on a sick friend."

"Oh, for—"

"Gunner, trust me, you don't want to talk to me right now. Talk to Fletch, set up a conference call at your convenience with the others, and I'll be there. But not now."

"Then you've made your decision?"

He'd made his decision before he'd even begun negotiations. "I'm close," he hedged, then handed the phone to Fletch. "Take care of this. You know where I'm going?"

"Yes, boss," he said.

"And don't follow me, okay?"

"You got it. I'll work on finding out about the Pharr-Rome connection."

He grimaced at that phrasing, but simply nodded, then left. After he went back upstairs to get shoes, he left the house and drove south. As he drove, he could feel his whole being tensing. Just the thought of seeing a slender, auburn-haired woman with incredible green eyes was making his palms sweat.

As he drove he realized that he'd felt so alone since last night, so isolated when he'd walked away from Margaret. The image of her lying on the bed was so painfully clear, it was as if she lay before him, her hair tousled, her lashes fanned on the golden tan of her cheeks. He raked his fingers through his hair, then slowed by the gates of the Pharr estate.

The closer he got to her, the more the sense of loneliness seemed to dissipate. Odd, but strangely expected. The gates were open this time, and he drove the Mercedes through and up toward the house.

MAGGIE WOKE TO SUNLIGHT streaming into the room, on a mussed bed, dressed in her shorts, halter top and a white terry-cloth robe. When she rolled over onto her back, she found out she also had a headache that made her head feel as if it were three times larger than normal. As she tried to swallow the cottony feeling in her mouth, she remembered everything that had happened before Fletch and Hill had freed them.

"Oh, God," she groaned. The agony filling her head matched the pain of the memory. She rolled back onto her side, tempted to just stay in that bed until she had a flight out to get off the island.

A knock on the door sounded like Big Ben chiming the hour, and she pressed her hands to her head to keep it from exploding. "Come in."

The door opened with an agonizing creak, and Pauline came into the room carrying a tray. "Good morning, miss. I trust you slept well?"

The woman looked and acted annoyingly perky. She hated "perky" right then. "Well," she muttered as she pushed herself up to lean back against the headboard. "I slept."

"Yes, miss." She put the tray on the table by the bed. "Oh, and happy birthday."

She'd all but forgotten about that. So, this was what thirty felt like. At least, this was thirty with a hangover and a lot of regrets. "Thanks."

"Breakfast?"

"Oh," she groaned, and pressed a hand to her stomach as the maid crossed and opened the balcony doors to let in the freshness of the early morning. "I don't think so. I could use some aspirin, though."

"Yes, miss," Pauline said, and was back at the bed, holding out her hand with two white pills resting on her open palm. "I brought these up for you. Are two of them enough for you?"

"Oh, bless you," Maggie whispered, and took the pills, then the maid handed her a glass of tomato juice. "Wonderful." She took the pills with the juice, then handed the glass back to the maid. "I can see why Amanda thinks you're so terrific."

The woman smiled but shook her head. "Miss, it wasn't my idea, it was Mr. McKay's. He left orders before he left last evening."

Maggie sank back against the headboard and drew her knees up to her middle. "Oh," she said softly.

"And he said to take care of your bump." She

leaned closer and studied Maggie. "It doesn't look very bad," she said, "but I could get—"

"It's okay. Don't worry about it."

Pauline hesitated, then said, "Miss, I'm sorry about yesterday, what I said and all, I had no idea that you knew the gentleman. I should have never said what I did about him."

"What did you say?" Maggie asked.

"You know, about women and him." She brushed her hands on the front of her uniform. "I'm truly sorry. I didn't know that you were seeing him."

"I'm not," Maggie said, cringing when the volume of her own voice made her whole head throb. "I'm not," she whispered.

"Of course, miss," the maid said. "When you're ready, breakfast is on the terrace." Then she turned and left.

When the door clicked shut, Maggie carefully eased off the bed, making no sudden movements as she made her way to the bathing area. Breakfast? The thought of food made her so nauseated she had to swallow twice before it passed. She went by the Jacuzzi and crossed to the huge shower enclosure. She stripped off the robe and her clothes, then stepped into the stall.

She turned on the water and stood very still as it ran over her, enveloping her with heat. Finally, she reached for a sponge and started scrubbing her body. As the sponge flicked over her chest, she froze, startled by the way images of Connor came to her. She gasped, dropped the sponge and leaned forward, pressing both hands flat on the tile by the showerhead and bowed her head.

You choose whom you love, you don't let love

choose you. He might be a billionaire, but that didn't make Connor McKay an expert on love. She hadn't chosen to love him, that love had chosen her. And it was a painfully irrational love, at that. A love that had nowhere to go and had to be lost. But she just didn't know how to do that. She didn't have a clue.

Maggie got out of the shower, scrubbed her hair partially dry with a towel, then decided to leave the bandage off her sore hand. The cut was closed and looked as if it was almost healed. One look in the mirror showed her that the bump on her head was almost nonexistent this morning. Just a touch of discoloration and a vague bump.

She dressed in clean denim shorts and a plain white T-shirt. When she went back into the bedroom, the air felt thin and the walls seemed way too close. Slowly, she walked barefoot down the stairs, through the silent house to the back French doors and out onto the terrace.

The day was fresh and lovely, and the ocean in the distance was imbued with a sense of peace that she wished she could grab and hold to herself. She crossed the worn stones to a glass-topped table with several dishes covered by silver domes sitting on it under a large awning. She lifted one dome, saw eggs and bacon, and almost dropped the silver topper. The next lid she lifted exposed toast and croissants.

She took a piece of dry toast, then crossed to the far side of the terrace to sit at the top of the steps that led down to a manicured garden. She sat on the stone, nibbled the dry toast and stared out across the gardens and lawn to the bluffs and the ocean beyond. Paradise. She never thought paradise would be like this. She felt a spasm in her stomach, and she pressed her hand to it, then took another bite of toast.

She was vaguely aware of soft chimes off in the distance, then she heard footsteps and turned to look over her shoulder at Pauline hurrying out of the house and coming toward her.

She looked up at the maid, who was grinning from ear to ear. "Oh, miss, you'll never guess who's here," she said in a slightly breathless voice as she reached Maggie.

Amanda. Thank God she was here. Maggie pushed her tangled hair back from her face and sighed. "This is so great." Relief was a wonderful thing. "Tell her I'll be right there, Pauline, or, better yet, send her out here."

"*Her,* miss?' the maid asked with a frown as she looked down at Maggie.

"Amanda. I can't believe she's finally here."

"Oh, miss, no, that's not who's here to see you. It's him."

"Him?"

"You know, the Ultimate Catch him," she said with a sly smile, stopping just before she winked. "Mr. McKay. He is so thoughtful, and..." She sighed as if at a loss for words. "He's here to see about you."

Her stomach gave a spasm, big time, and she hugged her arms over it as her headache roared to life. "Mr. McKay?" she whispered.

"Yes, miss. Shall I show him out here? Or do you wish to freshen up and receive him in the house?"

She turned to stare down at the steps below her as the twist in her stomach grew more painful. "No," she gasped. "No, don't. Tell him I don't feel well. I can't see him."

"Miss, I can stall him. You know, get him a drink or something?"

"No, I...I don't feel like seeing anyone right now."

"You're sure?"

She wasn't sure of much anymore, but one thing she was certain of was that she couldn't see Connor again. "Very sure," she said softly, and closed her eyes as sickness rose in her throat. "Just send him home."

"Yes, miss, of course," Pauline said, barely hiding the disappointment in her voice as she left.

Maggie buried her head in her hands and willed her whole being to settle down and relax. Just knowing he was in the house was playing havoc with her. With a low oath, she got to her feet and went farther down the steps, but she'd only gone down three steps before the sickness hit her with a vengeance.

She swallowed hard and wished she could die, right there and then. But that wish was far from coming true. Instead, she felt someone take her by her shoulders, and even before she heard him talk, she knew Connor was there.

Chapter Thirteen

"Good heavens, I didn't believe her," Conner muttered.

If Maggie could have, she would have twisted away and run, but she wasn't sure she could have run right then even if her life depended on it. She could do little more than let Connor ease her down onto the steps. Then she buried her face in her hands and swallowed hard again.

"Take a deep breath," he said to her, his arm still around her shoulders. Then he spoke to someone else. "Get some soda water, something with carbonation, and some dry crackers."

"Yes, sir," Pauline said.

She groaned and leaned away from him, resting her shoulder and arm against the wooden railing. "Don't say that...word," she groaned into her hands.

"What word?"

"The *F* word. Food."

He chuckled softly. "Pauline said you were feeling pretty rough, but I thought it was just one more of your evasion tactics," he said.

She grabbed the railing to her right. "I don't feel very good," she said with real honesty.

"You're hungover." He stated the obvious.

"I didn't think expensive champagne was supposed to do that to you."

He laughed again, the sound jarring her head, and she chanced a look at him. Thank goodness he was wearing dark glasses; at least she didn't have to deal with those midnight eyes when he grinned. As it was, her whole body weakened at the sight of him in a plain shirt and cotton slacks, forcing her to hold more tightly to the railing on her right.

"If you drink enough of any champagne, you'll pay for it in the morning," he said.

Then why did he look so criminally hangover-free and chipper sitting next to her on the step? His shirt was open at the throat, and she could see the pulse at the base of his neck beating steadily. "I guess so."

"Is this a good time to wish you a happy birthday?"

How did he know that? She couldn't remember if she'd told him or not. She grimaced. "I don't think so."

"Then I guess I shouldn't ask you how old you are."

"Not if you want to live," she muttered.

He laughed again and she cringed. "You can tell me when you feel like it, okay?"

"Perfect," she said.

Pauline returned, and Connor took a glass out of her hand and turned to give it to Maggie. "Drink this. Trust me, you'll feel better."

She took the glass and had to force herself to sip a bit, but as the cool liquid slid down her throat, she did feel better. A little more steady, at least, until she looked at Connor over the rim of the glass. The man was incredible. Just sitting there watching her, driving her crazy when he wasn't even trying to.

Slowly, he touched the bridge piece of his glasses and tugged it down on his nose so he was looking at her with those dark eyes over the top of the frame. "I could get in the habit of doing this," he said, his gaze holding hers intently.

Her stomach gave a spasm, and she quickly drank a bit more before resting the glass on her knee. "Doing what?"

"Playing doctor with you."

Damn those eyes and that grin. She couldn't begin to deal with them while she was in this condition. "Why are you here? To watch me be miserable?"

He pushed the glasses back in place. "That wasn't the plan. I just wanted to make sure you were all right."

"You can see how I am," she muttered as she gripped the damp glass.

"Yes, I certainly can," he whispered, and his fingers feathered across her cheek when he brushed at her wild curls that were falling forward, then skimmed over the bump. "Almost gone."

She held out her hand to him, palm up. "Almost gone," she said with a flourish.

"You're a quick healer," he said softly.

"Was there anything else?"

"Yes. I was going to tell you that you were wrong about something else, too, not just the champagne."

She'd been wrong about so many things, she couldn't pick just one to isolate. "About...about what?'' she asked, staring into the soda and the ice cubes floating there.

"About the sky diver."

She couldn't help looking at him. "What?"

"You said she was probably really nice and never thought about the money. Remember?"

The idea of women and Connor was making her stomach queasy again. "I remember."

"She's suing me for alienation of affection for having her arrested, and she's asking twenty million in damages."

"What?" she gasped.

He reached for the crackers that Pauline had left on a plate on the stair next to him. "Here, have one of these. You look pretty pale."

She grabbed a cracker and nibbled on it, but it didn't make her feel much better. "How can she do that?"

"Easy. She got a lawyer. Fletch found out from the papers this morning that the suit's been filed."

"Oh, my God, why would she do something like that?"

He shrugged as he took something out of the breast pocket of his shirt. There was a glint of gold in the sunlight as he flipped his lucky penny into the air, then caught it and held it out on his open palm to her. "This is why. This is what it all boils down to," he said.

Maggie stared at the coin on Connor's palm as Pauline came back. "Mr. McKay, sir, is she okay?" the maid asked.

Maggie watched Connor close his fingers tightly around the gold penny as he said, "She'll live. But it's going to be touch-and-go for a while."

The woman laughed, a sound that cut through Maggie's head. She grabbed the railing again, the idea of getting up and leaving very real, but she gave up on that thought when she felt her legs turn to rubber under her. She sat back, drank a bit more soda and knew she was trapped. She had to get Connor to leave.

"You'd better go," she said. "I feel like I'm going to be sick."

"Go ahead. I've got a strong stomach."

She sank against the rail. "Well, I don't, and I want to be alone."

"Alone in your misery?"

"Yes, in my abject misery," she said, then drank more soda. She stared down at the glass in her hand, at the fizzing water. "Then, after I'm good and sick, I have things I need to do. And you have work to do."

"I do?"

"What about that man you were supposed to call, Gunner, or whatever his name is?"

"He's mad. He didn't believe me when I told him I didn't call because I was locked in a wine cellar with a beautiful woman guzzling champagne."

Just the mention of their time in the wine cellar made her nauseated again. "I'm never drinking champagne again," she muttered, pressing the heel of her hand to her throbbing head.

His hand was on her shoulder, his fingers gentle on her skin and his voice close to her ear. "Love, never say never."

Maggie grabbed the rail with her free hand and tugged to get herself to her feet. She softly bumped Connor, then his arm was around her and she was steady, grounded, anchored. Everything she didn't want to be with him.

She barely had time to realize that the steady beating wasn't his heart, but running footsteps, before she heard, ''Hey, there, happy birthday to us!''

She turned to see Amanda at the top of the stairs, and even though she hadn't seen her for a long time, she looked just like the girl she'd shared a college dorm room with seven years ago. Slender, blond, in jeans and a loose top. A very welcome sight.

''Amanda!'' she gasped, and, pressing the soda into Connor's hands, she moved away from him. Using the rail for support, she went up the steps, meeting Amanda halfway. As they hugged, she whispered, ''A very happy birthday.''

Maggie was a bit taken aback to realize they were both crying. ''Oh, Maggie,'' Amanda whispered. ''I needed this.''

''Me, too,'' Maggie said, then drew back. ''I've missed you.''

She'd been wrong. Amanda was different, and not just older. The natural smile was gone, replaced by a tightness around her mouth and eyes, and when she frowned, a line cut between her eyes.

''God, Maggie, you're pale. You aren't sick, are you?'' she asked.

''I'm okay. I drank too much and...'' She shrugged. ''I'm hungover. That's all.''

There was a touch of the old smile right then. ''You started celebrating without me?'' she asked with mock reproach. ''What was it, Long Island iced teas?''

''Champagne.'' Connor was there, right beside her, but she kept her eyes on Amanda.

"Oh, champagne, a real celebration," Amanda said, her gaze flickering to Connor. "I'm Amanda Pharr." She smiled a bit more. "And you're our neighbor, aren't you?"

"Yes, I am. I just came by to see Margaret."

"Margaret?" Amanda said with a glance at Maggie. "You were that bad that he had to come and make sure you survived?"

"It's a long story," Maggie muttered.

"Well, I've got all kinds of time." She looked at Connor. "*Margaret* and I haven't seen each other for a very long time."

"Cousins?" Connor asked.

"No, sisters, but sisters by choice, not by birth," she said.

"Oh, okay," he said, and she didn't turn to see if he was smiling or frowning.

"That's a better way to get a sister. You pick and choose, you don't have one foisted on you," Amanda said as she turned and motioned to Pauline at the top of the steps. "Pauline, bring some iced tea out to the terrace, please."

"Right away," she said, and hurried off.

Then Amanda looked at Connor. "Join us?"

"He was just leaving," Maggie said quickly.

She sensed Connor give her a quick look, then he said, "I'll take a rain check on that. I've got business to take care of." As if he had every right to do it, he kissed Maggie on the cheek and touched her shoulder. "Happy birthday, love," he murmured, then went past Amanda with a nod and was gone.

Amanda cocked her head to one side and eyed Maggie narrowly. "Let's go and sit down before you fall on your face." She turned and led the way back onto the terrace.

As they settled at the table with the silver-topped trays, Amanda sat opposite Maggie and leaned forward, her hand outstretched across the table. Maggie sat down and took her friend's hand. "Now, *Margaret,*" she said with a smile. "Connor McKay? You? What's going on?"

"What do you mean?"

"When I saw the two of you, he was so close to you I couldn't see any daylight between you, and the tension was so thick, I could have cut it with a knife." The smile grew just a bit. "And Pauline said you'd been drunk and weren't feeling well. And the only thing I can think of that explains that sort of self-inflicted misery, is a man." She squeezed Maggie's hand. "And what a man, Maggie."

She drew back and pressed both hands flat on the cold glass tabletop. "Amanda, I don't think I want to talk about any of this right now."

Amanda sat back, crossing her arms on her chest. "Oh," she said.

"Oh, what?"

"Just 'oh.'"

Maggie shook her head. "Nothing changes. I haven't seen you for over seven years and you still do that."

"Do what?" she asked as Pauline set a tray with iced tea and glasses between them.

"Give me that look that says you know exactly what I don't even know I know."

Amanda laughed at that. "I do that?"

She wished they were in college and had no cares except what grade they'd get for their final exams.

Things had been so simple back then, but now life was all mixed-up. "You sure do. You always have."

Amanda pushed the glass of iced tea over to Maggie. "I've heard that Connor McKay has a strange effect on women, but never have I heard that he makes them sick. This is a new one on me."

Maggie ignored her glass of tea. "Amanda, can we shelve this? I'm going to have to leave tomorrow, and I want to spend my time catching up with you and celebrating our birthdays."

"You're leaving tomorrow? You can't. I just got here."

"I think I have to, but until then, let's just enjoy this." Maggie sank back in her chair. "Can you believe we're thirty?"

Amanda sobered. "It seems like yesterday that we were in college and that the whole world was in front of us. I really regret not seeing you since then. I meant to, but life just has a way of getting away from you."

"We saw each other at your wedding…at least, I was there among the thousands."

"Eight hundred people, and I knew only a handful. They were all John's friends and business associates." She took a drink of her tea, then set it on the tabletop. "I was lost back then. I should have realized that was a warning, an omen." She laughed, but there was no humor now. "I'm still lost."

"Amanda? What's going on with you? John called and he didn't even know about Shari being sick. He was looking for you."

"We're separated," she said bluntly. "And don't look so pained. I can't live with a man whose every waking hour is business. Every thought is of making money, when he has enough money for eternity, and he's never there for me or Shari. I can't do it any longer. I won't."

She was so calm, it was scary. "You don't love him?"

"I don't know. It's been so long since I felt anything, I just don't know." She lifted her glass toward Maggie. "Here's to fairy tales. Fun while they last, but they don't last forever."

Maggie felt her heart lurch. That was so true. "John sounded worried about you."

"John is only worried I'll be an inconvenience in his busy workday, or that his great family will say 'We told you so,' about me." She sat forward. "Enough of this. We're here to celebrate, to have a good time." She smiled, the expression a bit forced. "Let me unpack, get into a swimsuit and we'll take a swim, then talk and talk and talk." She stood and looked down at Maggie. "And, sooner or later, you'll tell me all about you and Connor McKay."

Maggie stood. "There's nothing to tell," she said.

"Come on upstairs with me and watch me unpack while you tell me all your secrets."

"I'll watch you, but there are no secrets."

Amanda studied her for a moment. "You never were good at lying," she said.

Only to Connor. "I've changed," she said.

"We all have, Maggie." She took Maggie by the arm. "Divert me and tell me something wonderful and wild and romantic."

That's exactly what she'd felt like since meeting Connor. It was wild, wonderful, romantic and impossible. "You asked the wrong person."

"Oh?"

"There you go again," Maggie said, smiling despite herself.

"I'll make you a deal. I need a diversion. I definitely need a diversion. So, this is the deal." Maggie paused with Amanda at the foot of the staircase that led up to the second floor. "I'll stop doing that if you tell me the truth about you and Connor McKay."

Actually, Amanda was probably the only person she could tell about Connor and have her understand. "Okay, but it's a long story," she said.

Amanda slipped her arm in Maggie's and led the way up the stairs. "Go ahead. I have plenty of time. Divert me."

"LET ME GET THIS STRAIGHT," Amanda said as she and Maggie lounged by the pool that afternoon. "He thinks you're one of 'them,' and you think if he knows who you are, he'd run like a scalded hound? Does that about sum it up?"

"Well, I wouldn't put it exactly like that, but I guess so." Maggie was lying on the lounge, the sun warm on her bare skin exposed by her skimpy bathing suit. Her sunglasses protected her eyes, but nothing protected her from the words of her friend.

"You lied. He believed you. He hates the common people lying to get to him, or at least a common woman trying to get to him. You're very attracted to him, and he's obviously taken with you. But you think that if you told him the truth, he'd dump you like yesterday's garbage?"

"Blunt but true," she said with a sigh. "If I wanted to, I could say this was all your fault, you know."

"My fault?" Amanda asked as she sat up in the

lounge next to Maggie's and cast a shadow over her. "What did I do, except invite you down here?"

She turned in Amanda's direction. "You told me to fit in, to pretend I belonged here, not to rattle any cages, or make any of the natives nervous. So I used your lie about being a distant cousin." She exhaled. "But it's not your fault."

"Thank goodness for that," Amanda said.

"The fact is, from the first, I didn't want Connor to know the truth. I still don't."

"Why not? He might surprise you and understand."

It was hard for her to say it, but she was totally honest with Amanda. "I'd rather just let it die when I leave than tell him and have him look at me like I was some lower life-form and think I did it all to just get to him."

"Sounds as if you've been running like mad since you met him, running away from him. That's not exactly chasing someone."

"He'd think it was a ploy. He's made it very clear that he doesn't trust anyone who's basically broke and outside his crowd."

"Snob," Amanda muttered. "Just like John's family. They don't trust anyone who isn't one of them. They think I was only with John for his money and family." She laughed, but it was bitter. "That's their mind-set, not mine. I don't want a thing from John except for Shari. I'm sure not one of them. I don't want to be."

She leaned a bit closer. "So, what's your plan? To pretend it never happened and go back home and marry Bill?"

She'd almost forgotten about her stomach, but it

did a flip-flop right then. "No," she said, pressing a hand to her middle. "I love Bill, but I'm not in love with him. I know that now."

"Oh."

"Amanda, for Pete's sake—"

"Sorry. That just slipped out from habit. What I meant was to ask you a question. Would you be interested in Connor if he was an assistant bank manager?"

Maggie winced at the question, but the answer was there, as easy as breathing. She'd love Connor McKay if he dug ditches. "Yes."

"You fell in love with him, didn't you?"

She could have lied. She could have refused to answer the question. But she didn't. "It doesn't matter."

Amanda leaned across to her. "Like hell it doesn't. If he loves you and you love him, how can you let it go? Just because you're worried about what he'll think of you? If he loves you, he'll know the truth when he hears it."

"Oh, Amanda, it's not that simple."

"I know. Nothing in life is simple. And you've always been so…" She motioned vaguely with one hand. "Even when you were told you were beautiful, you never believed it, did you?"

"I'm not beautiful," she said.

"See, what I mean? You're beautiful, intelligent, funny. Obviously Connor sees it."

"He thinks he sees a wealthy woman who's his equal."

"You are his equal. You just aren't filthy rich. And, trust me, that's nothing. You can have all the money in the world and it doesn't mean a thing if you're alone." She laughed a bit nervously. "Take a chance. Let go of good, solid, careful Maggie and see who you become."

Good, solid, careful Margaret. She cringed at that. That's the woman who would have gone back to William Rome, who would return to the library, and go back to a life that would have no Connor in it. And that thought was chilling. She could barely look at it squarely. She'd never been a risk-taker, but suddenly she felt as if she was on the brink of taking a risk that would change her life forever.

"If I tell him, and he…he walks away? What then?"

"Then nothing's changed. You'll leave, but you won't leave wondering 'what if' or regretting not trying. No matter what happens with me and John, I tried. No matter what his family thinks, I loved him for himself, not for his money, and, damn it, I tried." Amanda studied her intently, then said, "So, what is Margaret going to do?"

Maggie sank back in the chair and realized that something had been happening so gradually she hadn't been aware of it. When she'd kissed Connor in the water, she'd been another woman, a woman who wanted him, who needed him, who took a risk and who loved him. She'd become that woman and never knew it until that moment.

That realization was as terrifying as it was exciting. But she knew that there was no turning back now.

Amanda reached across the table to touch her hand again. "Good girl."

"What?" she asked, lacing her fingers with her friend's.

"You're going to talk to him, aren't you?"

"You're a mind reader, too?"

"No, I just know you. I know that under that careful and cautious exterior beats the heart of a wild and crazy woman."

Maggie laughed with Amanda, and it felt good. There was a sense of freedom in her now, and it was so very welcome. No matter what happened, she'd take a chance.

"Ma'am, I'm sorry to bother you,"

Pauline said as she crossed to the two laughing women. "But there's been a delivery for Miss Palmer."

"Are you sure it's for me?" Maggie asked.

"Oh, yes, miss, the man was very clear about that."

"What man?"

"Mr. McKay's assistant. Fletcher."

Amanda looked at Maggie. "Fletcher?"

"He's Connor's bodyguard."

Amanda stood. "Well, isn't this a nice turn of events. Let's go up and see what he brought."

Maggie followed Amanda back into the garden room and through the house up to the master bedroom suite. As they went down the hallway, Amanda said, "I'd say this is a sign for you. An opening for you to be honest with Connor."

It was one thing deciding not to walk away, but it was quite another to go to Connor and say, "I love you."

They stepped into Maggie's rooms, and there on the bed was a large gold box tied with a piece of white silk ribbon. Maggie crossed to it with Amanda right behind her. She stared at the box, all gold and beautiful, until Amanda nudged her in the back. "If you don't open it, I will."

She sank down on the side of the bed, then reached for the box. She was annoyed that her hands were vaguely unsteady as she unfurled the bow and lifted the lid on the box. "Oh, my goodness," she breathed when she saw, nestled safely in a bed of white tissue, the most beautiful feather mask she'd ever seen.

It was fashioned of gold feathers, embedded with glitter that caught and reflected a myriad of colors from the lights. It looked like something a person would wear at Mardi Gras, or to a regency ball. Elegant and lovely, large enough to cover the top part of the face, with slanted eye openings trimmed with tiny beads.

"Oh, it's beautiful," Amanda said as she reached past Maggie and touched the fine feathers. "Fantastic."

Maggie noticed a small card in the tissue and picked it up. She opened it, and in dark, sprawling bold writing that fit the man perfectly were the words "Happy Birthday. Connor."

Chapter Fourteen

"Why would he send this?" Maggie asked breathlessly.

"It's for the ball," Amanda said. "For the Sebastian Lake celebration tonight. It's a masked ball, some people in costumes, others with just masks. I'd say this will make our party very special. But that just leaves one question."

"You don't think I should keep it?"

"Oh, no, definitely keep it. I meant, the question of what one wears with a gold feather mask?"

"Amanda, I—"

"You're keeping it, and you're going to wear the perfect dress with it. I've got a clingy white gown that was made to be worn with it."

Maggie picked up the mask, then held it in front of her face and looked at Amanda. "What do you think?" she asked.

"I think," Amanda said as she reached out and gently drew Maggie's hand down, letting the mask slip so she could see her face, "that it's time for you to take off your mask for Connor McKay."

CONNOR HUNG UP AND SAT back in the chair in his office as the sun began to dip toward the horizon.

"We have met the enemy and he is ours." He glanced up at Fletch, who was feeding papers into the fax machine. "It's almost done."

"Gunner went for it?"

"He'll be begging me to take the company by tomorrow."

"What's the problem, then?"

"No problem. The financing's in place, Gunner's all but ready to sign. No problem. Why?"

Fletch shrugged. "Usually, when you get to this point, you're higher than a kite. You know, going in for the kill. But you look positively bored by it this time."

Connor knew Fletch was exactly right. He should have been high from the rush of the coming win, but right then something was missing. "Maybe I am."

Fletch frowned at him. "What's going on with you?"

"Damned if I know." He glanced at the clock. Four o'clock. It had been seven hours since he'd last seen Margaret. "That gift was delivered?"

"I delivered it personally as soon as it was finished, just before I came in to fax Stewart," Fletch said as he stacked papers on the desk. "Pauline said she'd make sure that Margaret got it."

He rocked back in the chair. "It's been an hour?"

"Maybe two."

The phone rang, and Connor looked at it. Had he been waiting for Margaret to call or to make contact in some way? He wasn't sure until the phone rang, then he knew it wasn't Margaret on the other end. Not on the business line. He motioned to Fletch to answer it.

Fletch nodded, then reached for the phone. "Mc-Kay Tech."

"Just a minute," he said, then lowered the phone and pressed his palm over the mouthpiece. "It's Belgium. They just heard about Gunner and need to find out about how the acquisition affects them. Something about lost jobs."

Damage control, something he expected he'd have to do, but not this soon. He took the phone, and for half an hour soothed troubled waters, explaining his plans and making sure that there wouldn't be any trouble with absorbing Gunner's European staff. He was aware of Fletch coming back into the room once, looking at him, then leaving. When Connor finally hung up, Fletch came back into the office.

"Done?"

"They're cool for now. Big excitement. Someone told them that the offices there were being closed down. Damn the gossips."

"You had a call on your private line while you were on with Belgium. Margaret Palmer."

Connor stood to face the big man. That's what he'd been waiting for. "Why didn't you come in and get me?"

"You were busy, and you know you hate being interrupted when you're doing damage control."

"Forget that. What did she say?"

"She wanted to thank you for the mask. She said it was beautiful and very thoughtful."

Connor crossed to the windows and looked out at the late afternoon. Right then, all the feelings he'd found missing with his dealings with Gunner filled him. There was a heady rush, a sense of completion that was staggering. She'd called. She'd made contact. Margaret wasn't running anymore. And over all of the feelings, he felt pure pleasure and an edgy sense of anticipation.

The woman never ceased to amaze him. She was nothing like any woman he'd ever met. She didn't cling, she didn't fawn, she didn't smother him. But she was there. She was always there, even when she wasn't around physically. She was in his mind and his soul.

He turned to Fletch. "What times does the party start over there?"

"Nine. Parties at the Fortress go till dawn most of the time."

"I need to get those figures out to Gunner as quickly as possible."

"I take it you're going to the party?"

"The deal's done, or at least, almost done, and I'll have time on my hands."

"Sure thing. I just have to worry about what I'll wear for a costume."

Connor crossed to Fletch and tapped the big man on the chest with his forefinger. "Go, have a good time, but know one thing. You're on your own. You aren't working tonight."

Fletch lifted one eyebrow. "I figured you'd be wanting space if you went."

"You figured right," Connor said, and went around to drop down on his chair and face the pile of paperwork. Annoying, boring paperwork that he couldn't wait to finish. "By the way, did you find out anything about William Rome?"

"Nothing yet, but I'm expecting Stewart to fax what he has soon."

"Good. Good," he said, then realized for the very

first time in a long time that he was looking forward to something besides work. And Margaret was at the middle of that anticipation. Yes, he was definitely looking forward to seeing Margaret at the party.

WHEN THE DOOR CHIMES sounded at the Pharr house at eight-thirty that night, Maggie was in her room just about to put on the dress Amanda had loaned her. The mask lay on the bed, side by side with the white dress, and Maggie was in her robe. But when she heard the sounds echo through the house, she had the strangest feeling that it was Connor, at the door.

He hadn't returned her call, but she found herself going through the house to the balcony that over-looked the entry. Pauline was there, rushing to the door to open it. But Connor wasn't there. John Pharr pushed into the house. He stopped in the middle of the foyer and turned to Pauline. "Where is she?"

"Oh, Mr. Pharr, we weren't expecting you, sir."

"Just tell me where my wife is," he said.

She remembered the John from seven years ago, from the day of his marriage to Amanda. But this man was different. The clothes were still expensively cut, from the tailored slacks to the custom shirt, but the happy, confident man from then had been re-placed by a man who looked distraught.

His dark brown hair was shot with gray, and his face, one Maggie had always thought of as almost *too* good-looking, looked haggard.

"She...she's dressing upstairs. Getting ready for the party tonight."

He turned before she'd finished speaking, and was going up the stairs two at a time. Maggie pulled back, but John spotted her and stopped at the top. "Maggie, tell me what's going on. I just heard that Amanda's filed for divorce. My God," he rasped as he raked his fingers through his hair. "I thought she wanted space, that she just needed time, then I find out she's filing for divorce."

The man looked horrible, desperate, and right then Maggie knew that Amanda and John were going to be fine. He loved her. Only a man in love could be that miserable. She could have almost laughed at her own thought, if he hadn't been in such obvious pain. "She's in her room, but she never said anything about a divorce."

He exhaled harshly. "She's filed," he said in agony. "Why in the hell didn't she talk to me?"

"I think she tried, but you were so busy and you weren't there."

He pounded a fist into his palm. "What a mess."

She went closer to him and touched his arm. "John, just talk to her. That'll be the best birthday present she could ever have."

He exhaled on a hissing breath. "Will she listen to me?"

"You have to try," she said.

He hesitated, then turned and hurried down the hall toward the master suite.

Maggie turned and went back to her room. Foolish to think Connor would come here, she thought, and she never expected John to be there. Life surely wasn't predictable. She took her time dressing in the gown Amanda had lent her. It was everything Amanda said it was, white, clingy and perfect. What she hadn't told her was that the back was almost nonexistent, the neckline was low and draped, and the straps mere threads of fabric.

Maggie looked at her reflection in the mirrors in the changing area. The woman looking back at her wasn't anything like the Maggie who had arrived here just a few days ago. It wasn't just the dress, or letting her hair go with its natural curl. There was something in her eyes, something that had never been there before. Not until she met Connor.

Nervously, she smoothed the fine fabric at her hips, then, after putting on simple makeup, she went back into the bedroom and picked up the bag Amanda had loaned her, a very tiny gold lamé purse. Then she reached for the mask and carried it with her out into the corridor.

The clock in the house struck ten, and still there was no word from John or Amanda. She got to the balcony and looked across it at the master suite area. She could see a light from under the main door, but she couldn't hear anything. She knew she was on her own for now.

She went downstairs and met Pauline, who was just coming from the back of the house.

"Oh, miss, you look lovely," she said as she clasped her hands together. "And that mask, it's so beautiful." She looked past Maggie as she got to the bottom of the stairs. "The missus?"

"She's still upstairs with Mr. Pharr. I'm going to go on ahead to the party. Could you call Marin with the car?"

"Oh, yes, miss, if you're sure you aren't going to wait for the missus."

"I think I should give her privacy, and I've never been to anything like this party. Could you just tell

Mrs. Pharr where I am, and if she can, to meet me there? If I don't hear from her or see her, I'll call for the car to bring me home.''

''Yes, miss. The car will be brought right around.''

''Thanks,'' she said as the maid went off to order the car.

She went out the front and down the steps, stopping at the bottom to wait for the car. She did want to give Amanda and John time alone, but she wasn't entirely selfless. She wanted to see Connor, and she hoped against hope that he'd be there. If he wasn't, she knew right then that she'd find him, either tonight or in the morning. She'd see him one way or another and her mask would be gone for good.

THE FORTRESS WAS transformed in the night. All the light outside the castlelike structure came from gas lamps on the walls, at the doors, down the entry and onto the drive that approached the front. The effect made the place look magical. As Marin pulled the car up to the entry, Maggie looked up the steps and had the oddest sense of understanding how Cinderella must have felt like going to the ball.

She smiled at that as Marin helped her out into the softness of the night, with the scent of blossoms sweet in the air. Music drifted toward her, mingling with the subdued sound of laughter and voices. It seemed surreal to Maggie as she went up the sweeping steps, put the mask on, and stepped into the Fortress.

Maggie wandered through the club, past ladies and men in full costumes of pirates, wenches, kings and queens, and some in elegant gowns and tuxedos. She mingled, refused champagne in favor of sparkling water, and by the time she made her way out onto the terrace, which had been cleared of tables for dancing, she knew Connor wasn't there.

She didn't know what she'd expected from the evening, but as the time passed, she knew it wasn't dancing with strangers who laughed and flirted, or standing by herself at the rail overlooking the dark waters. She glanced at a clock set into the stone walls and saw it would be midnight in fifteen minutes. She felt as if everything would turn into pumpkins and mice when the clock struck. This would all be gone, and the memories of Connor would be assigned to the realm of fantasies. The magic was slowly dissolving, and she had a feeling that there was nothing she would be able to do to recapture it.

But as she turned to go and call to have the car brought over for her, everything changed. Connor appeared right in front of her. And the magic was back full force, shimmering around the man in his dark tux with a band-collared shirt, gold studs and a look in his dark eyes that robbed the world of air for her.

All of the words she'd had in her, all of the ways she'd thought about talking to him were gone. Nothing was there but him in front of her, and the knowledge that she really did love the man. A man she'd just met. A man who could complete her world with a look or a word. Or destroy it. That made her tighten and the glow turned brittle.

What had she been thinking of? All of her resolve was dissipating, and she would have backed up, but the rail was behind her.

"I like it," he said in a voice so low she barely heard it over the music behind them, his eyes flickering to the mask. "I wondered if you'd wear it or throw it out."

"Didn't...didn't Fletch tell you I called to thank you for the mask?"

"Yes, he told me," he said. "But I never quite know what to expect from you." There was the suggestion of a smile, and her heart lurched. "I like that about you."

The man himself was unpredictable. "I didn't know if you'd be here or not."

"Actually, I would have called and asked you to come with me, but I wasn't sure if you'd accept or if you'd start running." He came a bit closer. "What would you have done if I'd called and said that I'd love to be able to take you to the ball?"

She looked up at him, and the truth came as easily as breathing for her. "I would have said I'd love to go with you."

The smile faltered. "I should have called," he murmured.

"Yes, you should have."

He shook his head. "You never cease to amaze me."

"Is that good or bad?"

"Very good, very good, indeed," he said softly, then reached out and stroked her cheek exposed under the bottom of the mask. "I'm glad you're here."

She trembled and tried to grasp at anything to break the knot of tension that was growing in her. "I thought you'd come dressed in a Sebastian Lake costume."

"No." He motioned down at his tux. "I chose someone else."

She didn't understand. "You aren't wearing a costume."

"Of course I am," he said, drawing back to flick the lapel of his tux. "Bond, James Bond," he said with a flourish in a perfect English accent.

The tension did break then, and she laughed, a bubble of humor that burst from her, and it felt lovely. She felt lovely. Everything was lovely at that moment. "Oh, of course," she said. "How silly of me not to know."

He touched her cheek again, pressing his palm there with a warm sensation that settled in her heart. "No, never silly," he whispered. "Never that."

She covered his hand on her cheek, the connection sure and wonderful and the intensity of her feelings for him overwhelming.

"Take off the mask," he whispered. "I want to see your face."

She let go of him and, with unsteady fingers, slipped the mask off. For a fleeting second, she felt naked in front of him. His eyes flickered to her lips, lingering there, then came back to meet her gaze. "I like this," he said, his smile as unsteady as she felt. "No hitting, no running." He took the mask from her and laid it on top of the rail, then reached out for her hand. "Dance?"

She didn't hesitate. "Yes." The strains of "Some Enchanted Evening" were everywhere as Connor held out his hand to Maggie. She put her hand in his, then he lead her onto the dance floor. As she went into his arms, she felt as if she had walked into a place she knew she'd been looking for all of her life. As if she was a part of Connor, as if her soul had merged with his, and, for the first time, she knew what it meant not to be alone.

She rested her head on his shoulder as they moved to the music; there was no awkwardness or hesitation in her. She moved slowly with him as his hand slipped to the small of her back, drawing her more tightly against him. Words would come later, she knew they would, but for now she just lived the moment, a new experience for her.

"You're like another person," he whispered against her hair.

That made her smile. "I am different."

"So, are you going to tell me why?"

She moved back a bit to look up at him, into midnight dark eyes. "I want to." She flinched at a sudden booming sound that echoed all around, followed by a shower of colors exploding into the heavens.

"Fireworks," Connor said as she turned in his arms. "It must be midnight."

Connor circled her with his arms, and she let herself lean back against him as a shower of blue and white flowed into the night sky, shimmering off the distant water, explosions of beauty, one following another, with barely a pause in between. She kept her eyes on the heavens, but all of her attention was centered on the man behind her, on the seductive way he swayed slightly with her from side to side, and the way he seemed to be surrounding her.

The finale came, a brilliant display of red, white and blue fire in the skies, then it was gone. The night was back and the music started again. She felt Connor resting his chin on her hair, then he spoke softly. "Are you going to tell me why you're so different?"

She could have said it right then, but she didn't

want to be here when she said it. "I...maybe we
could go somewhere private so I can explain."

"I don't know if I like the sound of that."

"I just need to explain something, but it's difficult
and I don't want to do it here."

He didn't ask any more questions. Instead, he left
her to cross to the rail and get the mask, then he was
back by her. "Let's go."

When he slipped his arm around her shoulders, she
went with him, back through the club and out into
the night at the entry. He handed a card to the valet,
and the man hurried off into the night. Neither of
them spoke until the Mercedes was there, then Connor helped Maggie into the car and went around to
get in behind the wheel. "Fletch isn't with you?"
she asked as she settled into the leather seat.

"He's here, but not with me," Connor said as he
drove away from the Fortress and the party.

Maggie looked at Connor through the softness of
the night, and the only light was the dull glow of the
dash lights. Shadows touched him, his features barely
a visible blue through the darkness. "Where are we
going?" she asked.

He cast her a slanted glance. "Where we can be
alone and not worry about being interrupted. My
place."

For a heartbeat she felt actual fear. Being alone at
his house. The idea was frightening. If he laughed at
her, if he rejected her, what would she do? Then she
knew. She'd leave. She knew the way up the road.
She'd done that before. The man was right that she'd
been running since the moment they met, but that
stopped right now. If she left this time, it wouldn't
be running away. It would be leaving.

Neither of them spoke again until they were at Connor's. He parked by a side entrance, then led the way into the house, through the house lit by soft security lights and into a dome-ceilinged room. High arched windows overlooked the terrace and the ocean in the distance.

There were couches grouped for the view, a massive fireplace on one wall and thick carpeting. Connor turned to her as he moved to the center of the room, and it felt as if the rest of the world didn't exist. "Okay, we're alone, and no one's going to interrupt us," he said. "Now, what's going on?"

She took a shuddering breath and clasped her hands tightly in front of her as she moved a bit closer to the windows. "I...I've been thinking and...I..." She shrugged and swallowed hard. It had sounded so simple. Just say it, but she couldn't get the words out. "Listen, I shouldn't...maybe I shouldn't be here."

Connor reached in his pocket and took something out. Then he walked across to her and held out the golden penny in front of her, caught between his thumb and forefinger. "A penny for those thoughts."

She stared at the gold coin, then he took her hand, opened it and pressed the penny onto her palm. Slowly, he closed her fingers over it, his body heat still caught in the metal. "No, you don't..."

"Yes, I do. I want to know what you're thinking." His hand closed over hers. "I want to know everything about you." He touched her with his other hand, brushing her cheek with the tips of his fingers, then trailing one finger to touch her lips. "I want you."

Maggie stared at Connor and the same words echoed in her. "Yes," she said breathlessly, and when he came even closer, she went to him…and initiated the inevitable kiss.

Connor never knew what to expect from Margaret, and this was no exception. Sending the mask had been a considered risk. He'd meant it when he'd told her that he hadn't known how she'd react to it. He hadn't.

When he'd found her at the ball, her back to him, framed by the softness of the night and the glow from the gas lamps, he'd almost not approached her. For a moment he'd thought it would be better just to watch her than to have her turn, see him and run.

But she'd stayed put. She'd actually smiled at him, let him touch her without jerking back, and when they'd danced, the change had been complete. He went with it, holding her, feeling her body against his, willing himself not to take her right then and there. The impulse had been so great that he'd welcomed the interference of the fireworks. Explosions in the air instead of inside him.

Holding her back against him, inhaling her scent, mingling her heat with his. Nothing could compare to that. Except this. Having her here, with him, alone, and her kissing him as if she'd been waiting forever for this. He knew he had been waiting an eternity for this moment.

He wanted her. The raw truth. An aching truth, that built and built as he tasted her and explored her. Aching desire consumed him, and this wasn't enough. Touching and clinging to her wasn't enough. He wanted more, much more, and he found the thin straps at her shoulders, easing them down until the fine material was gone and he touched her breasts.

Yes, skin against skin. Her breasts swelling to his touch.

He groaned as his desire consumed him. His need for her was a living thing, and as her nipples hardened and she moaned softly, almost animalistically, he knew that having Margaret was a matter of life and death. He moved to easily sweep her up into his arms, then as she clung to him, he went through the darkened house and up the stairs to the master bedroom suite.

Mary Anne Wilson

Chapter Fifteen

Connor wanted Margaret totally and completely, and he wouldn't take any chance of anything happening to stop him. He wanted her all to himself, and as he went into the suite, he kicked the door shut, closing out the world completely. She pressed her lips to his throat, and he realized that his tie was gone and the studs of his shirt were open. He didn't even remember that happening. Her lips burned against his skin, touching the pulse at his throat, connecting her to him in the most sensual way.

Then he was in the bedroom, and the next moment, he was with her in the big bed. He moved back from her, just long enough to strip off his clothes, then she held out her arms to him. In the moonlight that streamed in through the windows, he saw her. Incredible beauty. Her face lovely, her lips parted temptingly, her breasts swollen and arched up toward him. And then she was speaking in a husky, shaky voice that sent explosions of need through him.

"Please, love me," she breathed. "Just love me."

And he did. He went to her. Her dress was gone in a heartbeat, then there was nothing between them but the need that had taken on a life of its own. He was over her, her heat mingling with his, then her legs lifted and circled his waist. And he felt her against his strength.

He looked down at her, then slowly, with exquisite control, he slipped into her, into heat and velvety sensations that he'd never known before with any woman. She surrounded him, contained him, and the idea of becoming one with another person was very real. It was there. At that moment. In one heartbeat, Connor knew that no one else had ever experienced this. No one.

Her hips moved, and with a shuddering explosion of feeling, he thrust into her, deeper and deeper, and there was no control left. None. He went with her, the sensations agonizing and joyous all at once, then as she cried out, he went with her and the joining was complete. Together. Just the two of them. In a place where the world didn't exist. Nothing existed except this joining that was life and death for him. And he was exquisitely alive in that single moment.

MAGGIE WOKE SLOWLY to darkness and the sensation of Connor against her back. She lay very still, not daring to move, not wanting to move. She kept her eyes closed, feeling his body against hers, his thighs angled to match hers, his arm heavy around her waist, his breath tickling her neck and cheek each time he exhaled. And his heart beating against her back.

As each second passed, the sensations seeped into her soul. The slight ache in her from their lovemaking, the sense of urgency that had mellowed into a deep need that would never be satisfied. The man was gentle and demanding, urgent and patient, and he could make her feel things that she never even knew existed until him.

She felt something near her hand and touched it. The penny. Connor's penny. She touched it, then picked it up and held on to it tightly.

A clock chimed somewhere in the depths of the house, striking three times, and Connor stirred against her. He pressed his lips to her shoulder as his hand slowly moved to her breast, cupping its weight gently.

"You're awake?" she whispered.

"I have been for a while."

"Why didn't you say something?"

"I was thinking," he said softly against her skin.

"I've got your penny. I can give it to you for your thoughts." She felt him laugh slightly, his lips playing havoc with her against her skin.

"That's yours to keep," he whispered as his hand moved on her breast, catching her nipple between his thumb and forefinger. "I just want to know what you wanted to tell me."

She gasped as his fingers rolled her nipple slowly between them, sending shards of feeling deep into her being. "I...I wanted..." She took a shuddering breath. "I can't even think...if you..."

He rolled her over in one motion, and then he was over her, braced by one elbow on the bed. Even in the darkness, the man could make her melt with a look, all shadows and intensity. "If I what?" he whispered, his hand moving on her, slipping lower, over her abdomen, then lower still until he cupped his hand over her and she gasped.

She arched when he pressed against her, the heel of his hand moving slowly on her, making exquisite circles that made thinking impossible. "I...I...oh, Connor," she whimpered. "Oh, no."

"Oh, yes," he said on a groan, and she could feel him against her, swollen and hard, then he shifted and he was over her. His legs slipped between hers, then she felt him against her, testing her before he slowly slipped inside her.

This time the urgency was mellowed into a slow taking that formed a need as potent as anything had ever been in her life. Slowly, ever so slowly, that need began to consume her, to cause her to lose herself in Connor. She'd never be found again, but she didn't care. She wanted him with a passion that was terrifying.

She loved him. She loved him with a love that had no bounds, no limits, and when she felt the culmination of all that need and passion reaching its limit, she gave in to it. She went with it, higher and higher, until she was soaring with Connor, going to a place that was made for just the two of them.

Then she was joined to him, entwined with him, falling back and back until she settled into a soft, gentle place, where every wish was fulfilled and every need sated, and all because of Connor. As she drifted off to sleep, tangled with him in the huge bed, she knew that love might have come late for her, but when it came, it was so very real. So wonderful. Beyond what she'd ever thought it could be.

Connor kissed her forehead, then settled with a shuddering sigh. "Stay?" he whispered.

She snuggled closer, her hand pressed over his heart. "Yes, I'll stay," she said.

"Promise?"

"I promise."

CONNOR HAD NEVER WANTED any woman to spend the entire night with him. He'd always wanted to wake in the morning alone, but that morning, he shifted, felt Margaret there and sighed with relief. She hadn't left, and he was thankful. He never wanted her to be gone. He never wanted to wake without her. That settled into him, and he smiled. Damn it, it felt good to want someone with him forever.

A soft rapping on the door marred the stillness, and Margaret stirred. But she didn't waken. She shifted away from Connor, rolling onto her side, then settling softly with a sigh.

Connor eased away, took one last look at her, then drew the sheet up, resting it on her shoulder before he turned and reached for his robe. As he shrugged on the robe, he crossed and eased back the barrier. Fletch was there, still dressed in the clothes he'd worn to the party the night before. He had some papers rolled in one hand.

"This had better be good," Connor muttered as he held out his hand for the papers.

But Fletch didn't offer the papers to Connor. "It's the Geneva office. They're confused about the figures."

The last thing he wanted was to leave Margaret now. "Tell them to contact Harrison."

"They did, and they didn't like what he told them."

Connor hesitated. He glanced back at Margaret, snuggling into the bed, sound asleep, then turned to Fletch. "Okay, let's get this done," he said, and closed the door softly before heading down to the office. He hated the feeling of leaving her, and already missed her as he went down the stairs after the big man.

MAGGIE WOKE SLOWLY and luxuriously. She knew right away where she was and also that Connor was gone. She opened her eyes, looked at the bed by her, but it was empty. Pushing herself up, she realized she was still holding the gold penny. She looked down at it, then around the room touched by the morning light. He wasn't there. There was just emptiness around her, but she felt a connection with him from the penny. She closed her hand tightly around it.

Scooting to the side of the bed, she got up and padded across to the bathing area, but it was empty, too. She turned, spotted a stack of towels by the doors to a sauna and saw several robes stacked with them. She grabbed the nearest one and put it on. It fell past her knees, and the sleeves all but swallowed up her hands. As she went back into the bedroom, she knotted the tie and was startled by a knock on the door.

Before she could say anything, the door opened, but it wasn't Connor. Fletch came into the room, spotted her and crossed to where she stood near the foot of the bed. The man, dressed all in black, from slacks to an open-necked shirt, looked grim and not the least bit embarrassed to find her in his boss's bedroom next to a very messy bed.

"Good. You're awake" was all he said as he stopped in front of her. "We don't have much time, so let's get this over with."

She frowned at him. "I'm sorry. What's going on here? Where's Connor?"

"Working downstairs. He'll be busy for at least an hour."

He sent this man to tell her that? It made her feel uncomfortable, as if the night before was tainted somehow, and it brought a strange sense of wrongness to her. "I'm sorry, but I really would like to see Connor—"

He cut off her words with a terse "No."

She didn't understand at all. "What?"

He held out rolled-up papers to her. "It's all here."

She stared at the papers. "What's all there?"

He jerked the papers toward her, and his cold blue eyes were chilling as he spoke in a horribly controlled voice. "Margaret Marie Palmer. Thirty years old. Single. Librarian. Makes thirty-two a year. Dating an assistant bank manager, one William Rome."

Maggie felt her stomach knot.

"Margaret Palmer, former college roommate of one Amanda Clinton, who married John Pharr. Margaret Palmer, who wanted a life like her friend's. Who found out somehow, probably through the Pharrs' connections, that Connor McKay sometimes showed up down here. Who found a way to get to him, to connect with him." He exhaled with obvious distaste. "Sorry, it's over."

Maggie felt the blood drain from her head, and she reached blindly for the bedpost for support. "You're wrong, very wrong," she managed to say.

"No, I'm right. I've been through this far too many times with the boss to believe anything else. And you're out of here, lady."

This couldn't be happening. This man couldn't be doing this. "No, I need to talk to Connor." If she could just see him, if she could just explain. "I need to—"

"You need to leave," Fletch said pointedly as he tossed the papers on the bed, letting them scatter.

Maggie stared at the familiar pictures, some from the college yearbook with the captions still under them. Amanda's picture, a young, happy girl. "Amanda Clinton, cheerleader, drama club, tennis team. Goal—to be rich and have fun." Then her picture—one of the old Maggie—hair pulled tightly back from her face, with that look of bewilderment she always seemed to have back then. "Margaret Palmer, book foundation, chess club. Goal—to be just like Amanda Clinton."

"I was going to tell Connor," she breathed, then saw a single sheet that stopped her dead. It looked like a page from a tabloid newspaper, grainy and crude, divided by a lightning bolt down the middle of the page. And there were pictures she'd never seen under two headings: Pharr Heir Hit With Multimillion-Dollar Divorce on the left, and on the right, Ultimate Catch Might Be Caught.

Pictures she had never seen were spread out on the page. "Oil baron's soon-to-be-ex tutors friend in the art of landing a rich husband," read the caption under a picture of her with Amanda by the pool that had to have been taken just yesterday. The two of them in bathing suits, talking intently. Talking about Connor.

A picture on the other side of the page literally made her heart hurt. Connor and herself on his terrace when he'd been doctoring her hand. She was looking at him, smiling, and he was bent toward her, as if ready to kiss her. Below it, the caption read,

"Margaret Palmer puts lessons to good use by getting this close to billionaire Connor McKay, the Ultimate Catch."

"Oh, God," she groaned, and let the paper fall from her fingers. "I don't understand."

"Telephoto lenses offshore from boats. There's nothing to understand."

"But...I have to explain to Connor."

"No, you don't," Fletch said, and she looked into his face, cold and closed, his eyes biting into her. "Mr. McKay knows everything he needs to know. What you have to do is get the hell out of here."

Connor knew everything, and he'd sent this man to get rid of her? Pain clutched at her middle, and she flinched as Fletch took a step toward her. "You're not original, you know. Others have tried, but I'll have to say you got further than most." His eyes flicked to the bed, then back to her. "Now, do the decent thing and leave quietly."

Connor wanted her gone. That thought resounded through her and built pain in its wake. "I have to see him," she managed to say around her tightening throat.

"Look, this isn't easy for any of us, and I'm just doing my job, what I'm paid to do. Right now that job is to get you out of here. To make you all gone, to disappear without any more inconvenience for Mr. McKay."

Connor wanted her gone, and he didn't even care enough to come up here himself to tell her. He'd sent this man, and that hurt as much as anything.

"We can do this the easy way or the hard way," Fletch was saying. "I'll drive you back to the Pharr place, and you can let this die without a scene, or you can make a scene and force me to make you leave.''

A rock and a hard place. But her eyes were painfully dry. Even tears were denied her. She clenched her hands so tightly, she could feel the penny biting into her sore hand. That connection was still there. She knew it had to be.

As if reading her mind, Fletch spoke abruptly. ''If you're thinking of doing something stupid like confronting Mr. McKay, forget it. The last time this happened, he had her arrested.''

Maggie stared at the big man, and a part of her died. It was over almost before it had begun. A fantasy that dissolved into thin air.

''So, what's it going to be?'' he asked in that annoyingly calm voice.

She exhaled on a shuddering sigh. ''I'll leave.''

''Good,'' he said, and she could tell he was relieved. ''Get dressed and we'll go.''

''I can get myself out of here,'' she said firmly.

''I'll wait for you, and we don't have much time,'' he said as he got to the door and looked back. ''Hurry up.''

Maggie watched the door shut, then sank weakly onto the bed. She heard the crumple of paper and looked down at the tabloid page. Tears did come then, hot, scalding tears that blurred the horrible tabloid page on the bed. As she got up to get dressed and leave, she looked down at the penny still in her hand.

It was cold, so cold, as cold as all of her explanations felt. She turned her back on the pictures and the bed, got dressed, then as she stepped out of the suite, Fletch was there. He was obviously making

very sure she left without a scene. He walked with
her down to the entry and out of the house. As the
door closed behind them, he said, "I'll bring the car
around."

"Don't bother," Maggie said, and was thankful to
feel anger come to her rescue, at least for that moment. "But will you do one thing for me?"

"What's that?" he asked a bit warily.

She felt bitterness rising in her throat. "Tell Connor I won't sue him," she said. "He can keep all of
his money." With that, she handed the penny to
Fletch, then walked away from the world of Connor
McKay.

CONNOR WAS FURIOUS that it had taken him almost
two hours to break away from Gunner and his people. He finally slammed down the phone. He hurried
back upstairs, but when he stepped into the bedroom,
it was empty. Margaret was nowhere to be seen, and
one look in the bathing area and dressing room
showed that she wasn't there, either.

"Fletch!" he shouted as he went back into the
bedroom, and the big man was there before the sound
of his voice died out.

"Boss? What's up?" he asked as he hurried into
the bedroom.

"Margaret. Have you seen her?"

"She left about half an hour ago."

"She left?" He'd thought she'd gone swimming
or maybe was out by the pool. "Are you sure?"

"Yes, she left."

She was running again, but this time he wasn't
going to stand around and wait for her to decide to
come back or contact him. He went into the dressing

area, grabbed fresh jeans and a shirt, then came back into the bedroom and got dressed.

"Where are you going?" Fletch asked.

He zipped his Levi's, then shrugged into the white shirt. As he was tucking it into the waistband, he looked up at Fletch. "I'm going to find Margaret."

"No, you aren't."

He stopped with his shirt half tucked in and frowned at the big man. "What?"

"You don't want to go after her."

Fletch had never gone over the line where he told Connor what to do. Now he wasn't only telling him, he was actually blocking the way. Connor crossed to where his bodyguard stood. "What in the hell is going on?"

"I took care of the lady, and there shouldn't be any problems from it."

"God, what are you talking about? You took care of her? Why did she need you taking care of her?"

"I got rid of her for you. I was just coming to explain things to you."

"Good. Explain. And it had better be good," Connor said through clenched teeth.

He held out some papers he'd had behind his back until then. "Here. Read these."

Connor took the papers, unrolled them and scanned the top sheet, then the next and the next. He looked up at Fletch. "Where did you get these from?"

"I was checking. You told me to."

He looked down at the top paper, at a picture of a Margaret he barely recognized from what looked like a yearbook. "You sent her packing for this?"

"Boss, she lied to you. You would have never known about her if—"

"You think I didn't know?"

Fletch had the decency to look a bit taken aback. "You knew all of this?"

"I knew she wasn't rich. I knew she wasn't used to any of this. One look at her face when she saw the pool or when she was at the party, and it was a dead giveaway. How many women in these circles look enchanted by any of this? How many are impressed by warm champagne in a wine cellar?"

"She lied to you," Fletch said. "And she's been plotting with the Pharr woman."

"Plotting?"

Fletch reached for the papers, snatched the bottom one out of his hands, then held it up in front of him. "This. A huge divorce settlement for the Pharr woman. Getting the bucks from John Pharr, then dumping him." The tabloid page hung between them, pictures of himself and Margaret on the terrace. He remembered the exact moment the picture had captured, that moment with her hand in his, that smile on her face. God, he remembered. And he knew there was no guile there.

He also knew what she'd come to tell him. What he'd never let her say. He grabbed the paper from Fletch and crushed all of them in his hands. "This is trash."

"That doesn't change the fact that she lied to you. She set you up." Fletch motioned to the ruined papers. "William Rome is an assistant bank manager. She makes thirty-two a year."

"And?"

"And what? It was all lies. Don't you understand?"

He understood that he'd been blind. That if it had been anyone but Margaret, he probably would have given Fletch a medal for what he did. But now he was just sick that Margaret had had to face this man without him being here. "Even if everything you believed to be true was true, why in the hell didn't you just tell me about it? Why didn't you let me deal with it?"

"I didn't think it was important enough to bother you with when you had enough on your plate with Gunner and Brussels."

Was that how this man saw him? That business was more important than anything else? That chilled him, because it had probably been true…until Margaret. "Not important enough?"

"Boss, you've always said that in a deal, both people get what they deserve. She got what she deserved, and…" He glanced at the bed. "You got something for it. I called it even and told her to get out. You chased her until she caught you, and she was damned good at it, if you ask me. Just one more little gold-digging bit—"

Connor knew a rage right then that defied explanation, and he struck out. His fist hit Fletch in the jaw before he had any idea he was going to do it. The pain in his hand shot up his arm, and he pulled his fist back, clutching it with his other hand. "Damn you," he cried.

Fletch stood there, barely rocked by the impact of the punch, then he raised his hand and rubbed at his jaw. "I'll be damned," he whispered. "I had no idea."

"About what? That I could get violent if provoked?"

"That you really loved her."

Neither did he, not really, not until that moment. He loved her. "Now you know."

Fletch reached into his pocket and held out the gold penny to Connor. "She gave this to me and told me to tell you that she wasn't going to sue."

Connor took the coin and would have smiled, if he didn't have the distinct feeling that the sense of life and death that he'd experienced last night was a raw reality right now. His life was hanging in the balance, and everything depended on Margaret when he found her.

CONNOR STILL HAD the penny in his hand when he got to the Pharr house fifteen minutes later. He rang the bell and didn't realize how nervous he was until the door opened and Pauline was there smiling at him.

"Oh, Mr. McKay, good day," she said, and before she could say anything else, he cut her off.

"I need to see Miss Palmer."

The smile slipped slightly. "Oh, sir, she's gone. She left just a while ago."

Before he could ask her where Margaret was, someone was speaking behind her. "Pauline, I'll see Mr. McKay."

Amanda Pharr was behind the maid at the foot of the steps and as the maid moved back, Connor walked into the foyer. "I'm looking for Margaret."

"Why?" she asked with undisguised bluntness. "You threw her out, so why are you here?"

Connor raked his hand through his hair. "I have to talk to her."

"She doesn't lie, Mr. McKay, and she told me that you wanted her out of there, that you sent your flunky to do your dirty work." She came closer, anger burning in her eyes. "How dare you? Maggie never tried to do anything. In fact, she tried to stay away from you. She knew how you felt about the peons in this world, and she wasn't about to intrude into your life."

He wished he could deny it all, but he couldn't. "I have to see her."

"She doesn't need anything else from you."

Then a man was there, coming down the stairs and stopping just behind Amanda, and Connor recognized John Pharr. "Is there something wrong, Amanda?"

"No, Mr. McKay was just leaving."

"McKay? Oh, sure, I recognize you from the papers. What are you doing here?"

Connor didn't understand the way the man was touching his wife, the wife with whom he was supposedly in the middle of a bitter divorce battle. "I thought you and your wife were—"

"Divorcing? No, reports of our divorce are premature, about one hundred years premature, I hope. Made up by the tabloids, with help from my family, I'm sorry to say." His arm went around his wife and he held her close to his side. "Now, why don't you tell us just what you want with Maggie?"

"I need to see her. Where is she?"

"First, you tell me what you're going to do when you find her," Amanda said.

Epilogue

Maggie walked along the beach, heading south, and felt numb. She was thankful for that. The numbness. At least she wouldn't completely fall apart until she could get her flight off the island at two o'clock. Until then, she needed to move. She needed to keep going so she couldn't think or take the chance of that numbness slipping and her having to face what happened.

When she looked up, she realized that she'd gone farther than she thought, and she was almost to the cove. She didn't want to be there. Not in that place, but going back to the house and waiting wasn't an option. Maybe she could swim past the arch and get to the beach beyond and keep going.

She made her way over the rocks, scrambling for her footing, then she saw the arch, touched the side of it, and was about to wade into the water to swim across to the other side. She barely glanced into the cove, but what she saw stopped her dead in the knee-deep water.

A boat. A cruiser, Connor had called it. White and sleek, with bright blue at the water line. She stared at it, and wondered why no one had come for it. Had it been there since they were last here? That didn't make sense. She was very still, then without planning what she was going to do, she dove into the water and swam toward the boat anchored in the middle of the cove.

She stroked slowly, not at all sure why she was even going to it, then when she got within ten feet of its side, she knew she should have never done this. It wasn't abandoned. Not at all. Suddenly Connor was there at the rail.

She stopped swimming, treading water, and the sight of him looking down at her, his features defined by the clear sunlight, dissolved the protective numbness completely. It was gone, leaving agony in its wake.

"I wondered how long it would take you to come back here," he said.

"Oh, no," she whispered, and turned, stroking away from him as quickly as she could.

She heard the splash behind her and knew he was coming after her. She'd barely gone twenty yards before he was there, and he had her by the arm, stopping her in the water. She started to go under, but he had her, pulling her up as she swung at his hold on her. The impact was stinging and the connection was gone. But he wasn't. He was right in front of her in the water, those dark eyes with water-spiked lashes upon her.

"I left, what more do you want from me?" she managed to say, barely able to keep herself afloat with him looking at her like that.

"I want you," he said.

She knew that she wasn't hearing him right. She couldn't be. "Your shadow threw me out. And I left.

Didn't you get your message?'' she asked, anger completely taking over. ''I won't sue you for anything. I don't want your money.'' She bit her lip. ''I never did.''

She didn't know what she expected, but it wasn't him to say simply, ''I know.''

He was closer to her, and it was all she could do not to swim away. But she couldn't. Not until she understood. ''What? You know what?''

''I know that you lied to me, that you aren't a Pharr, and that you hated lying, that you were afraid that I'd hate you for it.''

''How did you…?''

''Amanda and John. They love you, you know.'' He was closer still, and his hand touched her face, brushing lightly at her wet hair. ''Oh, Margaret, I'm so sorry about all of this.''

Now she knew she was imagining things, that this had to be a product of some ancient spell or some sadistic ghost. ''No, no,'' she said. ''I'm sorry.''

His smile was crooked and so damn endearing. ''No, not that. Not matching apologies again. I can't take it.''

But she couldn't smile. ''But I'm not who you said you wanted.''

''No, you're not. Thank God. You're Margaret. My Margaret,'' he said breathlessly. Then he was closer still and his lips touched hers. But the contact was fleeting, teasing and tempting before he drew back slightly. ''I never knew what I wanted until you were there.''

''But I'm—''

''I know who you are, what you are. Do you think I could have been with you and made love with you if I hadn't known you and wanted you?'' He lifted his hand and opened it, palm up. The penny was there. ''This is yours. You forgot it when you left.''

Tears came, mingling with the saltwater on her cheeks. ''Oh, Connor,'' she whispered.

''Take it.''

She touched the golden penny and slowly took it into her hand. ''I never wanted it, you know that?''

''Hush,'' he whispered. ''Don't cry. Whatever Fletch told you, he thought he was doing the right thing. At least until I punched him.''

''You punched the human mountain?'' she gasped.

''Well, let's put it this way, I punched him, and the mountain didn't move. The thing is, he had no idea that I loved you.''

''Loved me?''

''Oh, God, love seems like such a weak word for what I feel for you.'' Then, amazingly, he looked uncertain. Connor McKay looked uncertain, almost uneasy. ''I just have to know how you feel about me.''

She drank in the sight of him, and a peace that the cove seemed to contain filtered into her. A peace that was only possible with this man loving her. She touched his face, her fingers unsteady. ''Oh, Connor, I love you, too.''

His smile was immediate and brilliant, and then he was kissing her. Together they drifted farther and farther down, lost in each other and the silence of the water, then they broke the surface and Connor was laughing. ''She loves me!'' he shouted, and the declaration echoed back over and over and over around them.

''I do,'' she said softly. ''I do.''

His smile faltered. "Save that thought, and say those words at the right time," he said. "Marry me, Margaret Marie Palmer?" His expression was so endearing. "They say I'm the Ultimate Catch."

"I won't marry the Ultimate Catch," she said. "But I will marry Connor McKay."

"Thank you," he said, and came closer again.

As his body brushed hers, she gasped. "You're naked."

"The lady's observant. That bodes well for our marriage, don't you think?"

"But what about those photographers?"

"Gone. Fletch ran them off. He's making very sure they won't be around this area for quite a while. So we have time."

He was against her, his hands manipulating the ties on her bathing suit, and in a moment the pieces of pink were floating on the water. Then his hands were on her, under the water, and she gasped.

"Oh, no," she said. "I...I dropped the penny."

His hand found her center and she gasped again, but he was smiling. "Well, you know what that means, don't you?"

She closed her eyes. "No."

"Diving for treasure. For gold."

"Oh, yes," she said breathlessly as he invaded her gently.

"Yes, indeed. But later, much later," he whispered as his mouth captured hers and they drifted down into the water, and Maggie knew that they had forever.

He's every woman's fantasy, but only one woman's dream come true.

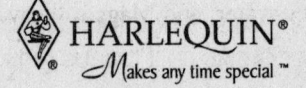